MW01255156

AVENGING ADAM

FBI-K9 Series

JODI BURNETT

Dedication

To all the K9s who risk their lives to save ours.

Avenging Adam

By
Jodi Burnett

Chapter One

Kendra's ankle crumpled under her in an awkward twist. Her knee hit the dirt, leaving bits of skin on the mountain path. The next victims were her palms, but she controlled her fall from there. She swung her hips around, landed on her butt at the edge of the trail, and sucked a lung full of fresh, pine-scented air in through her teeth.

"Ow—Shit!" Kendra brushed small rocks and sand from her scraped knees and assessed her ankle. Arrows of pain shot up her leg when she gingerly rotated her foot. She decided not to remove her hiking boot. At this point, she'd have to gimp back down the mountain as it was, and her boot would keep the swelling at bay for the time being.

Baxter, her bloodhound, sniffed her knee and offered her a cleansing lick. Kendra laughed and rubbed his head, flopping one of his ears up and down. "Thanks, boy."

On weekends, Kendra hiked the trails in the mountains above her home on the outskirts of Sedalia, a tiny town nestled against the eastern slope of the foothills in the Colorado Rockies. There was nothing better than putting a demand on muscles that during the past several weeks had spent too much time in a chair. Used to working search and rescue missions outside with her K-9 partner, her body was stiff from the computer research and phone calls her work focused on lately.

Kendra reveled in the peace and silence of the woods where the only sounds came from the wind tickling the tree tops, the tittering of Stellar Jays and, of course, the panting and occasional woof from Baxter. She relaxed in the realm of the deer, occasional fox, and scurries of chipmunks. The ripple of water as it tripped over stones in the small stream next to the path soothed away all forms of tension.

Baxter worked as her FBI K-9 partner Monday through Friday, but on the weekends he was her best friend and frequent hiking buddy. The US government employed him as a sniffer dog to find drugs, firearms, explosives, and missing people both lost or hiding. He was excellent at his job.

Baxter's tongue hung long and dripping out of his saggy jowls, as he sat down. He lapped up his drool with one swipe and resumed panting.

"Need a drink, buddy?" Kendra reached inside her pack for a water bottle and Baxter's collapsible bowl. After she poured him some, she splashed the rest of the water on her knees.

A breeze filtered through the pines and Baxter's head snapped up. He raised his muzzle to howl. He barked several times and then howled again before he sat. His eyes focused on something behind Kendra, and he barked again.

"What is it, Bax? What do you see?"

A low rumble vibrated deep in his throat before he let loose another set of barks topped off with a mournful yowl.

Kendra shifted and peered over her shoulder to see what had him so upset. Searching the forest behind her, she saw no one. She detected no wildlife either, though that wouldn't cause him to react so strongly. Highly trained, Baxter had better discipline than to make a ruckus over nothing. A slight warning tremor traveled across her skin, and her fingers automatically sought the firearm strapped to her hip.

Forgoing the wound cleansing and bandaging, Kendra pushed herself up to her feet, testing her twisted ankle. A sharp jab fired through the joint. She bit her lip and stifled a groan. Shifting all of her weight to her good foot, she stared once again into the trees surrounding the mountain path. Still she saw nothing, but Baxter was relentless with his alert.

Kendra hopped to the side of the trail looking for a broken tree branch, or something she could use as a cane to help her walk. She found a stick that was perhaps a bit too thin, but she tested a step or two. It was better than nothing, and she called out, "Seek, Baxter. Go get it."

Baxter took off into the trees before turning and sprinting out again to see if she was following him. He dashed back to his find and barked three times. He sat down and whined.

"I'm coming, Bax. Good boy." Kendra hobbled toward her dog. He'd found something he didn't like and wouldn't leave it until she checked it out and gave him the "free" command. The uneven ground made it difficult to traverse, but when she was a little more than halfway there, the distinct odor hit her before she set eyes on what Baxter was trying to show her. Death. Whatever it was, it hadn't been dead for long. It was a warm spring, so maybe a day or so—long enough to emit that sickly-sweet smell but not so long as to smell rotten and foul. Past a large pine, a woman lay on her back—not moving. Bile rose in Kendra's throat, burning and bitter.

"Good boy, Baxter." Kendra picked up her pace even as the pain seared her wounded joint. She approached the body tucked deep in the woods and knew it would be cold and stiff to the touch. The woman's skin held a waxy gray tinge and her open, slightly bulging eyes were vacant. The body wasn't bloated yet, another clue that the death was recent, probably within the last twenty-four hours.

Her fingers fumbled for the phone holster on her belt, and Kendra swallowed hard. She dialed 911. The cell coverage was spotty, so she limped over to an opening with fewer trees, cursing her bad luck of falling. Still unable to find a good signal, she pressed the off switch and volume button at the same time, hoping the emergency alert might get through better than an actual call.

Baxter growled and barked wildly. Kendra turned to see what had upset him but all she saw was a big log swinging straight toward her eyes. She dropped her phone and threw her arms up. She wasn't fast enough, and the wood smashed into her head with the force of a grand-slam home run.

———

"Yes sir. The victim bears all the evidence of similar attack wounds. I'm certain we have the same murderer on our hands. At least it mimics his MO, and so far we've kept several distinctive details out of the news. No way is this a copy-cat killer." Special Agent Rick Sanchez switched his phone into his left hand as the call transferred from his rental car to his hand-held device. He shoved the door closed. "I just pulled into the hospital parking lot. Hopefully, the agent who found the body has regained consciousness by now and can tell us something."

The Special Agent in Charge of the FBI office in Chicago's voice cracked over the line. "I'm sending the paperwork for your Assignment Transfer to the Denver headquarters right away. Call me when you know anything," he ordered.

"Yes sir. I'll keep you in the loop." Rick clicked off and headed toward the automatic doors of the Arapahoe Medical Park Hospital in Littleton, Colorado. The agent who hopefully saw the suspected killer, lay unconscious in a room upstairs. He'd met Kendra Dean last fall in Idaho at an FBI joint mission to take down a dangerous neo-Nazi compound. His partner, Jack Stone, had gone missing during a blizzard and Agent Dean had flown from Denver as part of a K-9 search and rescue team to help find him.

He and Kendra had shared an attraction, one he toyed with the idea of pursuing—but he lived in Chicago and Kendra worked with an FBI-K9 unit in Denver. That was the excuse he gave himself, anyway. Still, when he imagined connecting with her at some point in the future, he never dreamed it would be this way. Shit, he hoped she would be all right. Rick pulled his lower lip between his teeth as he crossed the hospital lobby. He was eager to find out what Agent Dean knew, but not so thrilled to share the bad news he brought with him.

Rick waited for the elevator and swallowed the sick swell creeping up his throat. He'd witnessed Kendra's connection to her sniffer dog, Baxter, during their mission. He was her first concern at every juncture. How could he face the injured woman with his sad news and then blast her with questions about the corpse she'd discovered?

A bell chimed before the stainless-steel doors slid open, bringing him back to the moment. He stepped into the compartment and rode up to the fourth floor. The agency posted a guard outside of Agent Dean's hospital room as a precaution, since no one besides Kendra knew who had attacked her.

Rick flashed his ID and badge. "She awake?"

The uniformed cop opened the door for him. "Not yet. Doc'll be here on his rounds soon though."

"Thanks." Rick entered the dark space. Light seeped in from the edges of the shades covering the window and mingled with the glowing screens of the monitors, giving the room a depressing pallor. A white gauze bandage covered the point of impact on Kendra's forehead. Dark half-moons stained the skin above her cheekbones where blood pooled, bruising both eyes. She'd look like a prizefighter when she woke up. If she woke.

Seeing her again, in person, even in her wounded state, reminded Rick why he'd been interested in her in the first place. She was beautiful in a simple, unadorned way. His chest tightened at her vulnerability, laying helpless in the bed. He pushed away the urge to run his fingers along her jaw, and instead he lifted her hand and held it in his.

"Kendra? Can you hear me?" He swallowed. "We'll catch the bastard who did this. I promise."

Rick's nerves jumped when a nurse silently slipped into the room and spoke from directly behind him.

"How's our patient this morning?" She reached around Rick and checked the IV bag. "Excuse me for a minute. I just need to check a few things, then I'll get out of your way."

Rick cleared his throat and stepped back. "No problem. When will the doctor be in?"

"Anytime now." She tapped on her iPad screen. "Are you a relative?"

Rick shook his head. "No ma'am, I'm Agent Sanchez, assigned to her case."

She gave him a thin smile. "I'll let the doctor know you're here. Does she have any relatives coming?"

"Uh, I'm not sure. I'll look into it."

The nurse nodded and left as quietly as she had come on her thick soled-shoes.

Rick pulled his phone from his suit-coat pocket and called the FBI Headquarters in Denver.

A soft, feminine voice answered. "Good morning, Denver FBI Headquarters, how may I direct your call?"

"Good morning. My name is Ricardo Sanchez, I'm a

special agent on transfer to Denver from Chicago. Will you please connect me with the K-9 unit?"

"Oh, hello, Agent Sanchez. We've been expecting you."

"Yeah, I'll be in later, but I wanted to stop by the hospital to see Agent Dean first."

"Sounds good. I'm Lucinda, the admin here. Looking forward to meeting you. Hold on a sec and I'll transfer you."

Rick walked to the window and peeked through the shades. The bright sun sparkled in a pure-blue sky.

"Agent Jennings, here." A sharp-cut voice echoed through his phone.

"Yes, Agent Jennings, this is Agent Ricardo Sanchez from Chicago. I'm assigned to the serial murder case connected with Agent Dean's discovery and subsequent attack."

"Hey, Sanchez. I got word about your arrival this morning. What can I do for you?"

"I'm at the hospital. Agent Dean is still unconscious, but the nurse asked me about family. Has anyone notified hers?"

"Yeah, her parents are in Missouri and she has a brother in Arizona. I believe he's on his way up. I think he arrives today."

"Great. Thanks. Listen, I'll be in the office this afternoon. Will you know anything more about Baxter by then?"

"I have a consult with his vet later this morning, but I don't think it's looking good."

"Shit. That's the last thing Dean's gonna want to hear."

"Yeah. Maybe best not to say anything until we know for sure what we're dealing with?"

Rick leaned back against the wall and looked up at the ceiling. "Right. Talk to you later."

"Let me know when she wakes up, will you?"

"You got it."

A tall man with gray hair fringing his scalp entered the room, followed by a woman in her late twenties scribbling on a clipboard. The man's gaze surveyed Kendra and then floated over to Rick. "Hello, I'm Dr. Wexley. How's our patient, this morning? Have you noticed any signs of her waking?"

Rick pushed up from his slouched position against the wall. "No, sir, I just got here myself." He held out his hand. "I'm Agent Sanchez."

The doctor shook it. "How do you do?" He referred to information on a laptop attached to a rolling cart. "I expect Agent Dean to wake up any time. She has a significant concussion, but the swelling is not alarming. Keep talking to her. Hold her hand. Gentle stimulation will help." He said something in Latin medical-ese to the intern following him like a magnet, before he pulled opened Kendra's eyelids, one at a time, and flashed a light into her pupils. "Good." He slid his penlight into his shirt pocket. "Call the nurse when she wakes up."

Rick rocked back on his heels and rested his hands on his hips as he scanned the group of monitors all beeping incessantly. He'd hoped to speak with Kendra this morning and then get to work hunting a killer, not sit around waiting in her hospital room. He hated hospitals with their antiseptic smell. Yet, in good conscience, he couldn't leave. Not until someone from her family showed up. He pulled a chair close to the side of her bed and sat.

"Come on, Dean." He took her hand, gently squeezing fingers tipped with short, unpainted nails. "Time to wake up. Baxter needs you, and I have work to do."

AFTER A QUICK STOP IN THE HOSPITAL CAFETERIA FOR A bland, dried-out turkey sandwich and a mini-carton of milk, Rick checked in with Kendra's supervisor. "Any word on the dog?"

"Baxter's out of surgery and in recovery. They had to take his leg."

"Shit."

"Yeah. How's Dean?"

"She was still unconscious when I stepped out about 30 minutes ago. I'm headed back up there now."

Rick stopped at the coffee machine next to the nurse's station to fill up before he entered Kendra's room. He nodded at the guard.

The officer stood. "Her brother's here."

Rick pushed through the door and introduced himself to a man about his same age, in his early thirties. "Any change?"

Michael Dean shook his head, his dirty blond hair showing no similarity to the rich brown of his sister's. "No. I've tried to talk to her. Even tapped her cheek, but nothing yet."

"Have you spoken with the doctor?"

"No. No one's been in." Worried eyes bored into Rick's.

"He came in earlier and seemed matter of fact. Said Kendra has a bad concussion, but the swelling isn't anything to worry about. He expects her to wake up sometime today."

Michael's shoulders relaxed, and he let out a long breath. "That's good to hear. I've always told her this job is too dangerous for her."

Rick tilted his head and considered the man. "You do know she wasn't working when she was attacked, right?"

"Whatever. Still."

Movement from the bed had both men rushing to Kendra's sides. She murmured, and a whimper slid out between her dry lips. Michael lifted her hand.

"Ken? Kendra? Can you hear me? It's Michael."

Kendra's eyelids flickered like she was blinking but her eyes remained closed. Michael's gaze shot to Rick. "Her fingers moved!" He turned back to his sister. "Kendra? Wake up, sis. It's me, Michael."

The pink tip of her tongue peeked out between her lips. "Mike?" The word breezed, barely a whisper.

"Yes. Ken, I'm here. I'm here and so is Agent Sanchez."

Kendra's forehead creased, and her lashes fluttered. "Wha —?" She moved her head and then grimaced. One eye opened a slit, the lashes sticking together.

"I'll get the nurse." Rick sprinted from the room to the nurse's station. "She's waking up!"

He returned, following a nurse wearing Tigger-print scrubs and purple Crocs, to Kendra's bedside. Michael was bent over the bed, whispering softly to his sister. He blinked and stood tall. "She's awake."

Rick peered around the nurse and met the pair of warm brown eyes he remembered from Idaho. The same ones that had appeared in his late-night thoughts during the weeks following the raid. Only now, smudges of purple surrounded them. He stayed back while the nurse checked Kendra's vitals and spoke to her. Michael held her hand and cooed encouragement. Yet those eyes pinned Rick to his place at the end of her bed. Finally, the nurse left to find the doctor.

"Baxter. Where's Baxter?" Kendra's first concern was for her dog.

Rick swallowed hard, and he clenched his jaw. "He's okay."

Her brows came together. "What happened?"

Chapter Two

Kendra blinked, her thoughts refusing to take concrete form. Michael hovered over her bed holding her hand, and Rick Sanchez stood next to him. *Rick Sanchez?* Why was a man she'd thought about often, but hadn't heard from in months—a man who lived in Chicago—standing next to Mike? At first, she imagined she was indulging in another fantasy, but that certainly wouldn't include her little brother.

"Michael?" Her voice sounded hoarse, and she cleared her throat. "What's going on?"

Her brother gave Rick a quick glance before he answered, and Kendra knew at once that something bad had happened. "Someone hit you in the head. You've been unconscious for almost twenty-four hours."

Kendra shifted her gaze to Rick. "Why are *you* here?"

A smart-assed grin flashed across his handsome face softening the sharp angles of his cheekbones. "That's not a very nice welcome after I flew all the way down here to see you. Did you miss me?"

Her eyes automatically tried to roll, and she regretted the

move instantly, closing them instead. "Why? What's happened?" Confusion spun her thoughts like a tilt-a-whirl and her stomach threatened to rebel.

Michael brushed some loose hair from her face. "You were hiking... do you remember?"

Kendra kept her lids closed and she concentrated. "Vaguely." Her mind refused to cooperate, and her tongue stuck to her throat. "Can I have some water?"

Rick reached for a lidded cup on her bedside table and held the straw to her lips. Kendra stared at him while she sipped. Her head screamed, and she was bone tired. All she wanted to do was drift back to sleep, but first she needed to know why Michael and Rick were here, together, by her bed. A sharp, painful jolt of clarity stabbed her brain, and her eyes flew wide open. *Where am I?*

"Am I in the hospital?" Panic surged along her nervous system and she struggled to sit up. "Where's Baxter?"

"Woah." Rick reached forward and pressed her shoulder back to the bed. "Don't try to get up. Yes, you are in the hospital, but you're going to be fine. You were hit in the head. Take it easy. Everything will come back gradually."

A whiff of his subtle cologne had her blinking at him. "You're really here. Why?" Her elevated heart rate set alarms off on two of the machines.

After the nurse pushed a few buttons to reset the monitor, she checked Kendra's pulse and took her temperature. "Gentlemen, I'm not sure what's going on in here, but Ms. Dean needs to stay quiet, and rest."

"Nurse," Kendra reached for the woman's arm. "What's happened? Why am I here?"

The nurse glared at the men before turning a kind smile on Kendra. "You have a bad concussion, but you'll be fine in a few days. The doctor will be here in a little bit." She turned to Michael and Rick. "You two need to keep her calm, or I'll have to ask you to leave."

"Yes, ma'am." Rick looked sheepish which caused a smile to twitch on Kendra's lips as the nurse left the room.

She rested back on her pillow and searched her mind for the recent past. "I hit my head? On what?"

Michael sat on the edge of her bed and took her hand again. "You were in the mountains up behind your house."

The memory refused to form. "Did you find me?"

"No. I flew to Denver this morning to be with you. The cops found you. Apparently, you called the police, and they tracked the GPS on your phone."

The throbbing in Kendra's head increased. "I called the police on my hike?" Her heart kicked up a notch, and she lifted her fingers to her forehead to press against the pain. She felt the bandage and looked at Michael in question. He shrugged, so she sought out Rick.

He held her gaze with dark eyes that didn't waver. Rick stepped forward and rested his hand on her blanket-covered leg. "You and Baxter came across a body. You called the police, but before you could report anything, someone hit you in the head. They tracked your phone, and when they realized you were an FBI agent in a remote area, they sent a helicopter to your location. They found you and brought you here."

Kendra's mind raced, and nausea overcame her. "I..." A regurgitative choking sounded from her throat.

Rick grabbed a plastic tub from the nightstand, dumped its contents, and held it in front of her, just in time. "Get the nurse," he commanded Michael, who hopped up and ran from the room. "Easy, now. You're okay." He held her hair away from the container.

Kendra nodded, wiped her lips and reached for her water

to rinse the sour taste from her mouth. Rick steadied the cup in her hand and helped her rest back on the pillow. "Thanks."

"No problem." Rick's hand paused on the side of her face and Kendra had to fight not to lean into his reassurance. She had to be strong on her own. He returned the tub back to the table.

"Where's Baxter? Was he hurt too?"

The muscles in Rick' neck flexed, and his Adam's apple bobbed. He cleared his throat. "He had to have surgery. He's in recovery now."

"Surgery?" Kendra scrunched her eyes closed and attempted to focus her thoughts. Her memory offered dark shadows, but nothing clear. "Why?"

Rick sat on the edge of the bed and took her hand. She was sure that was a bad sign, and she braced herself for the news. "Baxter was shot. He's going to be okay, but..." He pulled in a deep breath. "They had to remove his right, front leg."

Kendra's head spun. Colored lights whirled in a mist of white and she knew she would be sick again. The monitors tripped an alarm.

A cool hand covered her cheek, and at the same time fingers pressed against her wrist. A woman's voice chastised Rick for upsetting her. "That's it, you two need to go sit in the waiting room until the doctor comes. My patient needs her rest." The nurse herded the men away from her bed, and Kendra sat in silence wondering how Baxter got shot, and why she didn't remember any of it.

HOURS LATER, KENDRA'S STOMACH GRUMBLED A LOUD demand and stirred her from a deep sleep. Michael rose from his chair next to the bed and smirked at her.

"Hungry? That's a good sign." He reached for the nurse's

call button. "They told me to let them know when you woke up. Want something to eat?"

Kendra nodded and winced at the movement as she pushed herself up.

"Here's the control. Want me to raise the bed?"

"Yes, thanks." Kendra glanced around the room. She and Michael were alone, and Kendra pressed her aching head back into the pillow. "What time is it?"

"Past dinner. You've been asleep all afternoon."

"Water?"

Michael retrieved the cup and held the straw to her lips. "Mom and Dad want us to Face Time them as soon as you're up to talking. Maybe after you eat?"

"Was Rick Sanchez here?"

"Come on, Ken. Don't try to change the subject. They're worried about you."

"Are they?" Skepticism dripped off her tongue. Her adoptive parents rarely spoke to her unless they needed something. They weren't bad people, just disconnected. She was a disappointment to them whereas Michael was the golden child. She and Michael, though not related by blood, were the ones who looked out for each other. Michael had always been there for her.

"They *did* ask me to call."

"So call, and tell them I'm going to be fine." She raised her bed a little further. "So, about Rick?"

"Yeah, he was here. He left a couple of hours ago. Said he had to check in at the Denver office."

"Why is he in Denver? Did he say? Last I knew, he was stationed in Chicago."

Michael shook his head and backed away as the night-shift nurse entered to examine her. "You're looking more alert. How are you feeling?"

Kendra licked her lips. "My head hurts like hell, but otherwise..."

"That's to be expected. The doctor said we can give you some Tylenol with dinner if you're up to eating."

"I'm starved."

"I'll get you a menu from the cafeteria." She nodded and returned to the nurse's station.

Kendra smelled something spicy and tantalizing. Her mouth watered and her stomach rumbled. Paper rattled, and there he was.

Rick entered the room holding a large Chick-fil-A bag high in the air. "I brought you the food of champions." He flashed a grin, his teeth white against his brown skin. "Hungry?"

"You are now officially my hero." Kendra reached out for the paper sack. "I'm ridiculously hungry."

"I thought I heard your belly roar when I came in." Rick chuckled. "No way, am I gonna let them try to feed you the crap from the cafeteria." He pulled out a bowl of chicken noodle soup, and a chocolate shake, and set them on the bed table. "Don't worry, Michael. Plenty in here for us too."

Michael pumped his fist. "Yes! You're my hero too, man." He reached for a sandwich and clicked on the TV before settling into a padded chair.

The nurse returned with a paper cup holding Tylenol, and a menu. She raised her brows. "I can't argue that that tastes better than what they serve here, but how is your stomach handling the greasy food?"

"This is exactly what the doctor ordered." Kendra's spirits and energy lifted with each bite.

The woman handed Kendra the pills and set the list of cafeteria foods on the side table. "I circled a few foods that might help you heal faster. Blueberries for sure. Maybe order some for breakfast?" She reached for the remote control next to Michael and clicked the off button. "Also, absolutely no screens. That means no TV, phones, or iPads, until the doctor says it's okay. And no reading. Rest is the best thing for you right now." She turned to the men. "Don't stay too long."

They nodded obediently, and the nurse left.

Kendra swallowed a satisfying bite, and took a big gulp of the rich shake, before turning her gaze to Rick. "So—First, you are going to tell me what's going on with Baxter, and what the hell happened to us. Then, I want to know why you're here in Denver."

Rick nodded and finished chewing. "I stopped by your vet on the way here to see your pup, but he was still in recovery. They're keeping him sedated for a while, but the vet said the surgery went well. She told me most dogs adjust quickly to having only three legs."

Tears laced with what felt like acid pricked her eyes, and her bruised brain pounded. "What happened?"

"When he got shot, the bullet shattered the bones in his leg." The muscle in Rick's jaw flexed. "Thankfully, he survived."

"Oh my God." Kendra forced herself to look back. She remembered hiking. She'd fallen, twisting her ankle and skinning her knee. Absently, she reached for her injured leg, noting there was a bandage and an ace wrap. Shadows wafted across her mind as she struggled to remember more. "Baxter ran into the trees... he found..." Kendra stared at Rick. "He found something."

"Yeah." Rick leaned forward and waited for her to continue.

Kendra's heart marched and her brain echoed the militant rhythm. She closed her lids and pressed into the pain. "A body." Her eyes snapped open with the memory. "He found a body. A dead woman." She glanced at Michael. "That's when I called the police." She dropped her gaze to her lap and fought to remember more, but there was nothing.

"Right." Rick approached the side of her bed. "You sent an alert through your phone to the police. It connected and the recording sounds like you cried out, the phone dropped, and then silence. The cops found your phone under some foliage. It was crushed. Luckily, the GPS still pinged your coordinates."

Kendra searched her mind to no avail. "Did you identify the body? What happened to her?"

"I can only tell you what we think happened. First, we believe the woman was the victim of a serial killer I've been tracking for the past year." He glanced at Kendra's brother. "Hey, man. Can you give us a second? Some of what I'm going to tell your sister is classified."

"Okay." Michael stood to leave. "Hey, Ken. I'm staying at your place, if that's all right. I'll just head out there now and come back to see you in the morning. Get some rest." He narrowed his eyes at Rick. "Don't stay too long, and remember the nurse said not to upset her."

Rick gave him a curt nod. "I'll probably see you tomorrow." He pulled a chair to the side of the bed and sitting, he took Kendra's hand like he'd been doing it forever. "We've kept the details out of the press so we know we're on the right trail. The guy I'm pursuing kills his victims—all women —by strangling them. Often there are contusions to the face and torso, but he does not sexually molest them. The strangest, and most linking facets of his MO are that he removes his victim's lowest, left rib and crushes her skull with a rock. Two of the women, including the one you discovered, wore wedding rings and the ME found them jammed down their throats. Again, all of that is done postmortem."

"What? That is very specific—crimes of passion?" Kendra's mind stretched into the mist. She vaguely remembered the woman's body, lying on the ground, on her back. She leaned her head to the side. "There was no blood on the woman I saw. Her clothes looked clean."

"Yeah. By the time the cops got there, that was no longer the case."

"What do you mean?"

"I believe you and Baxter interrupted the killer's routine. He was probably there to smash her in the head and get his rib—what I've come to think of as his form of a trophy. When he saw you, he knocked you out with a fallen branch. Baxter must have tried to attack him." Rick brought his other hand up and held hers with both of his. He looked at the floor between his knees. "Your firearm was not in its holster when the cops found you. We think the killer took your gun and shot Baxter. Once you were both out of the mix, he cut the woman's rib from her body, hit her head and disappeared."

Weight pressed down on Kendra's lungs, making it hard to draw in a breath. She searched Rick's almost black eyes. "He shot Baxter with my gun? That son-of-a-bitch has my gun?"

"There was nothing you could have done, Kendra. You were unconscious."

"But why?"

"I assume Baxter tried to attack him. I'm certain of it."

"No, I mean, why didn't he kill *me*?"

Chapter Three

❧❧❧

Kendra's question haunted Rick all through the night. The mattress in his temporary housing was too soft, and the pillow was lumpy. Even on a regular night, he might not have slept well, but with all the facts of the case running through his mind, he didn't have a chance. He rolled off the edge of the bed and stumbled into the bathroom to get ready for the day.

Why hadn't the killer murdered Kendra? She was an easy target, lying there unconscious. Once the killer shot Baxter, he could have taken his time. The fact that he didn't had to mean that the dead women all had something in common that Kendra didn't share. *But, what?*

Obviously, all five were female, but they came from different parts of the country. Two were married, three were single—three of the women were white, one black, and one Hispanic. As far as Rick's research showed, none of the victims knew each other or went to the same schools. There had to be some connection. Something he was missing—but what?

Rick toweled himself off after he stepped out of the

shower, then wiped steam from the mirror. He wrapped the towel around his waist and lathered the black stubble on his face with sandalwood-scented shaving cream. Dark eyes stared at his reflection, struggling to come up with answers. With each stroke of his razor, Rick listed the rest of the details he knew.

One, as far as they could tell, each victim had gone missing, most likely abducted, during the daytime. Two, all the bodies were found in the woods or wilderness. Three, none of them were sexually assaulted. Four, all had their lower, left ribs cut from their bodies and their skulls crushed, post-mortem. Five, two of the women—the married ones—had their wedding rings pushed into their throats.

Six... "Shit!" Rick nicked his jaw as his mind wandered to Kendra and the thought of her lying on the ground vulnerable to a psychotic killer. He splashed his face with hot water, stuck a piece of tissue on the cut, and pulled clothes out of his suitcase. Instead of his usual suit, today Rick dressed in jeans and hiking boots.

On his way to the south side of town, he stopped at Starbucks. Breathing in the roasted coffee-bean laden air, he ordered a venti dark-roast and a muffin. With his caffeine and blueberry breakfast in hand, Rick drove to the veterinarian to see Baxter.

He followed a vet-tech back to the recovery kennels. "How's he doing?"

The young woman peered into Baxter's kennel. "He's still groggy. The doctor is keeping him mildly tranquilized so he won't try to do too much too soon. Did she give you the post-op instruction packet?"

"No. I'm not his handler." Rick squatted down to check on Kendra's dog. He lay on his good side with the bandaged amputation elevated. Baxter's droopy eyelids opened a slit and his gaze rested, unwavering on Rick until he was too tired to keep his eyes open. "Poor guy. I bet he's confused."

"It will be better for him when he can see his person."

"Yeah, she's in the hospital too." Rick stuck his fingers through the gate and touched a soft brown paw. "Your mom is okay, buddy. She'll come get you as soon as possible."

Baxter sighed out a whine on his next breath, but he didn't open his eyes. Rick snapped a photo for Kendra before he left, allowing the dog to rest.

His next stop was the Sedalia Sheriff's office. The local sheriff had offered to drive with him on ATV's up the mountain to the spot where Kendra found the body and was subsequently attacked.

Kendra's brother called while he was driving and told him that he was taking Kendra home from the hospital after lunch. *Maybe, she'd let me bring dinner over tonight.* Rick was anxious to know if Kendra remembered anything else. His best hope was that she'd seen the killer's face, but so far, she still didn't remember much.

THE CRIME SCENE INVESTIGATION TEAM HAD ALREADY GONE over the area with minute precision. They recorded all the evidence, had it bagged, and removed, but Rick wanted to have his own visual image of the scene. A knot of yellow crime tape trapped at the crook of a branch was the only sign left that anything unusual happened there.

The sheriff walked him through the wooded area where the dead woman was found, the location where Baxter had been shot, and finally to the matted down area where Kendra lay, unconscious, while a crazed killer mutilated a dead body a mere twenty feet away. Rick knelt and ran his hand over the dry grasses in the flattened spot. Green shoots of spring pressed up underneath the crushed foliage. A shudder coursed through Rick's shoulders at the thought of what could have happened.

He took photos from several angles, his phone's click-and-buzz loud in the silence of the day. Rick let his mind place the victims in the scene. "Anyone have any idea how the killer got the body up to this remote location?"

The sheriff stuffed his hands in his pockets. "No sayin'. He could have driven her up here on a vehicle like ours. There were no scuffs near the path, so we assume he carried her back into the trees. She was probably already dead, cuz there were no struggle marks in the dirt underneath her body, or the ground by her shoes."

"I wonder if Agent Dean interrupted him in the act of..." Rick didn't complete the thought about the rib. The ribs and crushed skulls, along with the wedding rings, were bits of evidence he held close to the chest. But still he wondered if the murderer left and then came back later to take the bone. *And if he left, where did he go?* "Have any of the townspeople seen any strangers hanging around lately? Maybe rented a property to someone, or something?"

"Not that I've come across so far." The sheriff spit tobacco into the dirt. "It's hard sayin' 'cuz folks from the city drive out here to the trailheads all the time. We're not that far from Littleton, or Denver for that matter."

Rick ran through the locations of the previous dead bodies in his mind. The first one was in Tennessee, up near Dale Hollow Lake, about 120 miles from Knoxville. The second and third bodies found with both missing ribs and bashed heads were the victims that brought Rick into the investigation. One of them was discovered in Wabash County, and the other in Perry County, both in the southern tip of Illinois.

The small town of St. Francis, Kansas was where they

found the fourth body. She had been left in a field near the Kansas-Colorado border. The missing ribs and shattered skulls were the evidence that indicated a serial killer was on the loose and garnered the interest of the FBI. Now, in a tiny berg outside of Denver, they'd found victim number five with blood-caked hair, a missing rib, and a wedding ring lodged in her throat.

"Has anyone come forward and identified the body yet?" The sheriff interrupted Rick's thoughts.

"Yes, I believe the husband identified the body, though I'm not sure what all has been disclosed at this point." He took one last long look at the scene and climbed onto his ATV. "Let's head back. Thanks for bringing me up here."

"No problem."

Next stop was the Denver Bureau Headquarters. It was time to gather all the case notes in a single location. Rick determined to find this sick son-of-a-bitch before he killed any more women.

Chapter Four

✿❦✿

Rick pulled his newly assigned black Explorer up to the address he'd entered into Google maps. He parked at the curb and studied the modest brick house with its tidy yard and garden. A large lilac bush burst in full bloom at the corner of the bricked-in front porch, but no other flowers stretched up to greet the spring. A precisely trimmed privet hedge stood sentinel on either side of the steps. Kendra's property, which Rick estimated to be approximately three acres, snugged up to the foothills on the western edge of Sedalia.

The drive from the Bureau offices in Denver had taken him over an hour, but he imagined her commute was worth it for the view alone, not to mention the small-town atmosphere. The place seemed to suit what he knew of Kendra Dean.

Balancing two large pizza boxes in one hand, Rick pulled himself out of the car and started up the walk. He lifted his fist to knock, but Michael flung the door open before he could.

"It's about time, I'm starved." He held open the door. "Kendra doesn't have any real food in this house. Did you bring beer?"

Rick chuckled and nodded to a six-pack hanging from the hand he balanced the pizza on.

"Thank God." Michael took the bottles from him and motioned to the table. "Hey Ken, Rick's here with food." He removed two longnecks from the cardboard beer caddy and put the rest in the refrigerator.

Rick crossed the front room to a small dining table that separated the living room from the kitchen and set the boxes down. He accepted a beer from Michael, popped the top, and savored the cold malt and hops blending on his tongue.

Kendra appeared at the opening to the hallway off the kitchen wearing an oversized T-shirt and sweats, covered by a worn, flannel robe. She leaned against the doorjamb. The heavy bandaging on her head had been exchanged for one large gauze pad. The purple and blue that encompassed her eyelids and pooled under her eyes had darkened. By tomorrow there would be a tinge of green.

"Hey, Rick. Thanks for bringing dinner, it smells amazing. I don't know how much longer I could listen to Michael whine about not having any junk food." She flashed her brother a tired smile and sniffed the Italian spiced aroma.

"Why don't you sit down. Don't you need to keep your ankle elevated?" Rick pulled out a chair. "You still look weak. Are you sure you should be out of the hospital? I thought the doc said he wanted to keep you until tomorrow."

Michael scoffed. "I tried to tell her that too, but Kendra insisted on going home."

"I'm *fine*," Kendra countered. "I can rest better at home than at the hospital, anyway." She slid into the chair and Rick pulled another one over for her foot. "The plates are in the cupboard, over the dishwasher."

Michael lifted a slice with thin strings of cheese drooping down, still attached to the pie. He took a large bite. "Who needs plates?"

Kendra closed her eyes and shook her head while Rick schooled his expression to neutral. He agreed with Michael in general, but Kendra was the type who craved order, and since he was her guest, he obediently retrieved the dishes. "What do you want to drink? I imagine beer is out of the question for a while."

"Water's fine. There's also veggies for a salad. Michael?"

"Pizza's good for me." He lifted a second slice.

Kendra let out a long breath. "No doubt, but would you please make a salad for Rick and me?"

"Ken, men don't eat salad with pizza and beer." Michael winked conspiratorially at Rick and tossed himself on the couch. He clicked on the TV.

Again, Rick agreed with him in principle, but figured Kendra wanted something green along with her dinner. He opened the refrigerator and found a variety of produce.

"Thanks." Kendra limped into the kitchen, pulled out a cutting board and two knives. She stood next to him and together they made a colorful salad. Rick smiled to himself at the homey scene and their rhythmic chopping. They worked together, side by side, with no need for words.

"You should be sitting down." He nudged her with his hip.

"I'm not putting any weight on my sore ankle and besides, I've been sitting all day."

"Still. You look tired, come on." Rick helped her to the table. He set the salad bowl in the middle.

Michael called from the couch, "Hey, sis. Can you grab me another beer?"

Rick drew his brows together and glanced at Kendra. She started to rise, and he grabbed her arm. "No. I'll get it." Rick took Michael a cold one from the fridge, but when Michael reached for it, he pulled it back. "Hey, man. Don't ask your sister to serve on you. What's the matter with you?" Rick set the beer on the coffee table. "Isn't that why you're here?" He picked up the remote and clicked off the TV.

Michael gaped at him. "Whatever, Dude."

What a prick. Rick joined Kendra at the table. "You haven't been taking care of him all day, have you?"

Kendra gave him a vague shrug and a wave of her hand.

A small flame ignited deep in Rick's chest. Guys like Michael pissed him off. He ground his molars together, swallowed his irritation for the time being, and brought Kendra a glass of ice water.

"Don't mind him." Kendra drizzled dressing on her greens. "He's always been a bit spoiled."

"When's he going home?"

"Tomorrow. Mike has to get back to work, and I'll be fine on my own."

Rick wiped pizza sauce from the corner of his mouth. "Good. Maybe you'll get some rest then. You can call me if you need anything, and I'll stop by after work with dinner. How about steaks?"

A soft smile lit Kendra's bruised face. "That sounds great, but I'm not your responsibility either. I can manage just fine on my own."

Rick raised his hands in surrender. "I have no doubt about that, but you're currently my only witness, so I need to keep an eye on you. When you feel up to it, I have questions."

Kendra sat up taller and faced him. "Shoot."

"No way. Not tonight."

After they finished their meal, Rick collected the plates and cleaned up the kitchen. "Hey, Michael. Why don't you come with me tonight? You can stay at my condo. That way you'll be a good hour closer to the airport in the morning."

"That'd be great. I'd save bank on Uber." Michael glanced at Kendra. "Ken, would you mind if I left tonight?"

Rick was sure he glimpsed relief in her eyes before she dropped her gaze to her hands. She covered a yawn with her fingers. "I'll be fine. I'm just going to sleep, anyway."

Rick gripped the back of her chair. "Come on. Let's get you into bed now, before you pass out at the table." He helped her stand and walked with her down the hall to her bedroom.

At her door, she turned to face him. "Thanks for dinner, and for taking Michael."

"Sure." Rick leaned against the doorframe. "I don't like the thought of you being out here alone, but at least you'll be able to rest."

"Yeah." Kendra smiled up at him.

He resisted a sudden urge to brush her hair out of her eyes and jammed his hand into his pants pocket. "I want you to call my cell if you need anything." His gaze moved from her eyes to her lips where it lingered for longer than appropriate. He snapped his eyes back up.

She searched the depth of them before she said, "You'll be clear across town. Don't worry about me, I can always call my neighbor if I need to."

"That's good." Rick couldn't seem to make his feet move. It was time to go, but he hesitated.

"Okay." A smile played on Kendra's lips. "I guess I should get to bed."

"Right." Rick smiled at her. "I'll see you tomorrow, then." Still his steps were slow.

"Will you have Michael come say goodbye before you two leave?"

He nodded and forced himself up from her doorjamb. Rick passed off his magnetic reaction to her as mere concern for an injured co-worker. Certainly, his draw to her was because of her connection with his case.

"See you tomorrow." Without meaning to, he leaned forward and brushed a kiss against the soft skin of her cheek. The action surprised them both. He pivoted abruptly and walked down the hall. *What the hell is wrong with me? No way am I going down this path again.* "Michael, your sister wants you to go say goodbye to her. I'll be waiting in the car."

Ten minutes later, Michael sauntered out the front door and leapt down the steps. He slid into the passenger seat. "Thanks for this, man."

"It's no problem." Rick started the engine and pulled away from the curb.

"Plus, it gives me a chance to talk to you."

Rick frowned. "What about?"

"Kendra. Listen, I'd appreciate it if you would help me and our parents to convince her to change jobs. She's not FBI material, you know? Ken's too... fragile."

Rick kept his eyes forward but his brows knit together. "I don't know what you're talking about. Kendra's a terrific agent. She's smart and intuitive, and her training will keep her safe."

"Yeah? How safe did that training keep her last weekend? She could have been killed."

"That would have happened to anyone hiking on that trail at that time. It had nothing to do with being in the FBI."

"Still, her fabulous training didn't help her any. We'd just prefer she did something she was more suited to."

Rick couldn't believe what he was hearing. "I can't agree with you, Michael. I don't know Kendra all that well, but I have worked with her in the field and found her to be highly competent, especially in search and rescue. I think she's perfectly suited to her job."

Michael glared at him and sat quietly for several miles

before he spoke again. "Okay, then. I hope you'll at least stay away from her. She should have men in her life that are concerned about keeping her safe."

Rick shook his head but kept his mouth shut. Nothing he could say would make this any better. Clearly, Kendra's family didn't understand how much she loved her job nor did they have any idea of the talent she displayed as an agent.

Chapter Five

The next morning, Kendra donned her darkest sunglasses, so as not to exacerbate her headache, and she drove to the vet clinic to see Baxter. She probably shouldn't be driving so soon, but she wasn't on any heavy medication, and the clinic was only a few miles away. The house felt empty without her dog. Kendra tried to imagine Baxter with only three legs. When she called, the vet reassured her that with time and some specific exercises, Baxter would adapt well to having only three.

Kendra's pulse hammered as she entered the clinic and approached the reception desk. A woman with over-teased hair spoke on the phone, but waved to let Kendra know she'd seen her. The receptionist adjusted her sweater before pushing a clipboard with a stack of paperwork attached to it, across the counter. Kendra took a seat in a hard, plastic chair and began filling in the forms.

The vet, with her long, straight, black hair pulled into a ponytail that swung across the back of her lab coat, came through the door into the waiting room. "Agent Dean?"

Kendra stood. "Yes, that's me. How's Baxter doing this morning?"

The vet smiled. "A little better each day. I think he'll make a quick and full recovery." She held the door open for Kendra. "Why don't we go to my office and chat about post-op procedure and what you can do to assist his rehabilitation? There are a few items you'll want to have on hand before Baxter comes home, and I'd like to instruct you on caring for his incision. With diligent nursing, Baxter should be fully healed within two to three weeks."

"So soon?"

"Animals are incredibly adaptable. As long as he doesn't overdo it or develop an infection, yes, it should be that soon."

Kendra shifted her weight onto her good leg. "How different will things be for him at home? I mean, do I need to have any special equipment? What about walks, or hiking, when he gets better? Will there be limitations?"

The vet offered her a kind smile. "We'll send you home with everything you'll need for pain management and wound care. For the first couple of days, Baxter will have to wear a cone on his collar, so he can't lick or chew his bandages off. After that, if you have an old T-shirt, you can slip that on him and tie off the arm of the missing leg. That will be more comfortable for him and still prevent him from licking his incision." The doctor lowered her gaze and tapped a pen on her desk. "I'm sorry to say that Baxter will have to retire from the K-9 team. He'll live a healthy, happy life, but that type of strenuous activity is in his past."

Kendra bit down hard, holding in a sob that worked to push its way out. She knew this was their new reality, but hearing the words out loud stung. Closing her eyes, she nodded.

The vet stood and held her hand out pointing in the direction she wanted Kendra to go. "For today's visit, we'll keep Baxter in his kennel with the door open. We don't want him to get too excited or try to walk just yet. So, keep him calm."

Kendra clenched her fingers into fists and wrapped her arms around herself as she moved toward the animal recovery area. She didn't want to do anything to cause Baxter more pain and worried he'd try to jump up when he saw her. Dog barks echoed from a distant room as the vet led Kendra to his kennel.

Instead of leaping up, Baxter merely whined and thumped his tail twice on the floor. A heavy mixture of love laden with remorse flowed from Kendra to her heroic dog.

"Hi buddy. Hi, boy." She sat on the tile in front of the cage and unlatched the door. A big wet tongue lapped her fingers when she reached inside to stroke Baxter's velvet wrinkles. "I hear you saved my life." Tears welled when Kendra gazed at the place where a hairy, brown leg should have been.

Baxter whined again and nuzzled her hand. Kendra glanced up at the vet. "He's so sleepy."

"We're keeping him slightly sedated so he doesn't tear out his stitches. I'd like to keep him here for another week, for observation and to manage his sedation during his initial healing. I encourage you to visit as much as you can. You both need to learn how to be with each other in a new way."

Kendra nodded, but couldn't answer past the rock wedged in her throat.

THAT NIGHT RICK SHOWED UP WITH STEAK DINNERS HE'D ordered for take-out and picked up at The Outback. He arranged their meals on plates and sat across from her at the dinner table.

"You look like you're feeling better today. Have you been able to rest?"

Kendra smiled. Not only had she rested but she also had a shower, and that had helped. "Yes, and I went to see Baxter today."

Rick narrowed his eyes. "Did someone drive you?"

She rolled hers. "No. I did just fine."

"You're not supposed to be driving yet."

"I wore dark glasses and drove slow. The vet is super close. It was no big deal."

Rick stared at her for what seemed like a long while. "How is Baxter?"

She shook her head and shrugged. "He's doing better than I expected, but it's so sad to see him without his leg. I wish I could explain things to him. He must be so confused."

"I'll bet he was glad to see you."

A cozy warmth spread through her. "Yeah. We were both happy about that."

"How's your memory of the day you were attacked? Anything new?"

"Honestly, I think I remember everything. The problem isn't a faulty memory, it's that I never saw his face, so I can't remember it. I remember everything up until I saw the wood coming toward my head."

Rick sighed, clearly disappointed. "Okay. Do you mind going over that day for me, one more time?"

Kendra started at the beginning of her hike and told the story for at least the tenth time. There was nothing new.

"So, you didn't see any blood on the body when you first saw her?"

"No."

"The killer obviously came back later to do the bodily damage of crushing the skull and stealing the rib." Rick went on, catching Kendra up on the details of the case, filling her in to see if she had any further insight than what he'd already come up with.

After dinner, they played Gin Rummy. Rick refused to play anything with her that used too many brain cells. Kendra knew he was being overly-careful, but didn't argue too hard as long as he stayed and kept her company. She loved the feel of her home with him in it, and it was nicer than she thought it would be to have someone around. Even if the company was kind of bossy.

"Gin." Kendra claimed and laughed.

Rick elevated his eyebrow at her skeptically.

"Did you order any dessert?"

"Dessert? Man, you're needy." He gathered the cards and shuffled them.

"That's right. I am."

"Sorry, no sweets."

"That's okay. I have ice-cream in the fridge." Kendra smiled innocently at him.

Rick laughed. "Oh, you do, do you? And I suppose you want me to get you some?"

"Yes, please. It's Mint Chocolate Chip—my favorite."

"Mmm. That's good, but not as good as double chocolate fudge. But, since you're losing at cards, I guess I'll get you some."

Kendra laughed, loving the easy feeling of being with him. "You're losing. Not me."

"Nope. I'm definitely winning." He winked at her on his way to the kitchen.

IN A SURPRISINGLY SHORT AMOUNT OF TIME, BAXTER HAD learned how to navigate with three legs. In super-dog fashion, he was always happy to see Kendra come through the door, and wagged his tail with enthusiasm. Kendra hated that he had to wear a cone around his head. The contraption was more difficult for him to figure out than the missing leg. At one point, he ran the edge of the cone into a door frame and knocked himself off his feet.

"Be careful, Bax." Kendra's heart wrenched as she helped him get up. Tears soaked her voice. "Don't worry, you won't have to wear this stupid thing much longer."

They took short walks around the clinic together and Kendra learned to clean and re-dress Baxter's stump with the vet's supervision.

Finally, it was time to take him home.

With Baxter in the house, Kendra felt strong enough to face her mom, so she propped up her iPad to FaceTime. She thought of herself as independent and capable until she talked with her adoptive parents. She was grateful to them for giving her a good life and she loved them, but somehow, they always managed to take the wind out of her sails. Kendra knew she should call them more often, but it could be days before her confidence recovered from a long visit with them.

"Hi, Mom."

"Kendra, I was wondering when you'd call. I know you've been resting a lot, so we waited for you. Look at your face." Her mom's soft round cheeks drooped as she peered at the screen.

"I'm doing fine. I just brought Baxter home from the vet hospital today."

"Michael told us they had to amputate his leg. We're so sorry. I hope you'll come to your senses and stop all this FBI silliness now. You should move back home where we can take care of you."

A heavy sigh pressed out from Kendra's chest. "My job with the FBI is not silly, Mom."

"Well, Michael agrees with us. You know, you could always

move down to Arizona and be closer to him if you don't want to come home."

"Colorado is my home now."

"But there's no one there to take care of you."

An angry weariness wrapped itself around Kendra's shoulders. "Why is it, you refuse to believe that I can take care of myself? I'm a grown woman—a trained agent in the FBI, for God's sake."

"Now see, sweetheart, there you go getting all upset..."

TIME CRAWLED BY. NEITHER KENDRA NOR HER DOG WERE good at sitting around. Baxter seemed impatient with his healing process, and Kendra worried that he'd hurt himself if he ran about too soon, but he was determined. She spent the morning researching training and care for dogs with amputations. All she found out was that her vet was thorough and knew what she was talking about.

Kendra was equally squirrelly about taking time off work to rest. Her head was fine, and she hardly felt any more pain in her ankle. She wanted to get back to the job. Dan Oxley, SAC of the Denver Headquarters, called her that morning and after they negotiated, he relented. Instead of the two full weeks she merited, he agreed to make it one. But, when she came back to work, he ordered Kendra to spend some time at the headquarters building helping on active cases there, where he could keep his eye on her.

She didn't really have much of an argument since Baxter couldn't return to work and she didn't have another dog to work with yet. Kendra consoled herself with the thought of working in the same space as Rick. If nothing else, he'd be nice to look at while she did her time. If she played her cards right, maybe Oxley would assign her to Rick's serial murder case. After all, she'd taken one for the team already.

Twelve tabs deep in her current research, Kendra surfaced when she heard the doorbell. She wasn't expecting anyone, but occasionally one of her neighbors stopped by. They rarely spoke, only waving to each other when they drove by, but out in the country, your neighbors were always there for you when you needed them.

"Coming." She called out as she closed her laptop. Kendra opened the front door to a cheerful bouquet of huge sunflowers. "Oh, wow!"

Rick stood behind the flowers and poked his head around the blooms. "Hey. I thought you could use some cheering up. I know you're going stir-crazy."

"These are so pretty. I love them. Thanks." Kendra reached for the vase. "Come in." She turned to find a good spot for the bouquet.

Rick stepped in after her. "Oxley told me he's forcing you to stay home for the rest of the week."

"Yeah, I tried to get him to let me come in earlier, but he was firm. At least I'll be back in one week instead of the original two."

"I do have some good news. He's assigned you to my team. You'll be working with me, Cameron, and Stott."

Kendra gestured for Rick to sit on the couch. "That's great news. Burke Cameron is a friend of mine. I don't know Stott very well, but I hear he's a good egg. Can I get you a beer or something?"

"Sure, thanks." Rick sat down on the sofa.

Kendra went to the kitchen, snagged two bottles from the fridge and dumped some potato chips into a bowl. She brought the snack to the living room.

"How's the head?" Rick accepted his drink.

"Hurts a little if I over use my eyes. I understand the rules but it's almost impossible to live without looking at stuff."

Rick looked at the MacBook on the coffee table and raised questioning eyes to her.

"I know... I know, but I'm trying to learn everything I can about taking care of Baxter now."

"Be careful, Kendra. You don't want to have any permanent damage."

"Yes, Mom." She smirked.

"I'm serious. You've got a week, so take it." His gaze darted around the house. "Where's Baxter? How is it having him home?"

"He's in his kennel. I'm supposed to keep him as still as possible for a few more days."

"How's he doing?"

"Really good. He's so brave. It will take some time before he completely adjusts though."

"I can only imagine."

"So... it was really nice of you to drive all the way out here to bring me flowers. It's not like I'm on your way to anywhere." The gesture meant a lot to Kendra, but she wondered about his motive. He hadn't tried to touch her, let alone kiss her since her first night home. She would have welcomed it if he had, but maybe he wasn't interested in starting a relationship. He lived in Chicago, after all. Who knew how long he'd be in Denver? She'd be happy if he stayed, but it was more important to catch the killer.

"It's not a bad drive, when I plan around rush hour, and I don't have anything else to do. I don't really know the area very well, yet."

"Well, if there isn't anything better to do, then..." she teased.

"That's not what I meant." His smile hinted at a dimple.

"I know. I'm happy to have the company too. It gets pretty quiet out here."

"I imagine, especially if you're not reading or watching

TV." He gave her a look filled with skepticism, and she laughed.

"I try to behave, but it's harder than you think. Since you're here though, we could watch TV and I'll promise to close my eyes and only listen."

"How about I take you to dinner and we just talk? I think that's okay for your brain."

"Can we get ice cream for dessert?"

"Do you always negotiate?"

Chapter Six

The day finally came when Kendra was allowed to
return to work and she approached the blue-glass
FBI building. She pulled open the doors, scanned
through security, and strode across the inlaid FBI emblem
toward the elevators. Glad to be back at work, she hummed
to herself while she waited. Impatient energy zipped through
her system from the top of her spine, across her shoulders,
and down through her bouncing heels.

She had agreed to put in only a half a day and it had to be
at the main office. She was on temporary medical leave from
the K9 team and no one wanted her to return too soon.
Baxter wouldn't be returning at all. A dull ache throbbed
behind her sternum. Kendra was thankful he was alive and
that she could keep him at her house, but she would miss Bax
as a work partner. And she wasn't at all ready to think about
training with a new dog.

Baxter was home in his luxury outdoor kennel. The
government provided the dogs with custom heated and air-
conditioned digs. Only the best for the K9s. Kendra was torn.
She desperately wanted to be back on the job but she worried

about Bax, so the short day suited her. She'd visited her dog every day at the vet clinic for the past week and learned how to help him adjust to his new way of living.

She worried about him being home alone, but a rush of warmth comforted her heart, pushing away the dread. Her sweet boy was her hero. All the first responders on the scene said they were certain that Baxter had saved her life by distracting the killer. Tomorrow she'd bring Baxter into Denver with her. The K9 unit was holding a small ceremony in his honor.

Ding.

The elevator doors slid open and Rick stood inside the compartment waiting for her. Her breath caught as she took in his swarthy good looks. The collar of his white dress-shirt stark against his bronze skin. Kendra loved a man in a suit. So many guys went casual these days, which she thought was a shame. Rick's almost black eyes held hers and the air sparked between them.

He'd come to her house every night since she left the hospital. Rick spent a majority of that time getting Kendra up to speed on his serial murder case. She couldn't deny a certain magnetism between them, but it was bad timing. They had to remain professional if they were going to work together. Not to mention that Rick's status as the lead agent on the serial murder case at the Denver office was only temporary.

"Good morning," she chirped. *God, I sound like a high school cheerleader.* Kendra cleared her throat.

"Morning." Rick grinned, his teeth flashing white. "Welcome back, Agent Dean." He stretched a hand out to keep the elevator door from closing. "Today's the big day, huh? How's Baxter doing? Will he be okay at home alone?"

"He's doing surprisingly well." She stepped into the compartment. Rick stood close enough for her to smell his subtle musk and she breathed him in. "It's great to have him home, but I'm glad to be back at work too." She punched the button for the third floor. "How's the case going?"

"Slow. I'm beginning to wonder if the guy's even still in Colorado or if he's moved on."

The elevator doors opened again, and another clean-cut agent who kept his blond hair trim and combed neatly to the side met them. "Welcome back, Dean."

"Thanks, Cameron."

"You sure you should be on the job again, so soon? I heard they were giving you a couple of weeks."

"They did, but I only took one. I'm fine."

He nodded at her before his gaze riveted on Rick. "Sanchez, there's been another murder. Body found west of Chatfield Reservoir. Same MO."

"The victim was strangled?" Rick stepped off the elevator.

The junior agent bobbed his head. "Affirmative."

Rick took the folder Cameron held out to him. He opened it and scanned the contents, his gaze pausing on the blood-soaked hair. He read further. "Missing lower left rib. Shit."

The men turned in tandem and walked toward a pool of cubicles leaving Kendra to follow behind. She dropped her purse off with Lucinda at the reception desk as she walked by, rushing after them. Rick strode into a glass-walled office and slid into the chair by the desk, never taking his nose out of the case file. A panoramic view of the front-range served as a backdrop to his workspace. *What the hell? How does Sanchez rate this office? He's only on temporary assignment.* Kendra tamped down the prickly green ooze that tried to choke her. She'd dreamed of an office like this someday, but not until she retired from fieldwork.

She took a leveling breath and bent to read the papers on Rick's desk, upside-down. "This our guy?"

Rick looked up at her and blinked. "I think so." He glanced at his watch. "Cameron, I want you and Stott to go interview the victim's family and friends. We'll rendezvous back here at four o'clock." He turned to Kendra. "Let's go. I want to see the crime scene before they remove any evidence." He closed the folder. "Call the local PD, or whoever has the area secured, and tell them not to touch anything until we get there."

Seriously? Do I look like a secretary? "I'll pass that on to Lucinda. Have you met her? She's our admin." Rick lifted his gaze to her and his black brows followed suit. Perhaps her tone was slightly on the bitter side of tart, but she was an FBI field agent, and not one Rick Sanchez could order around. *Give the man an office and he thinks he's in charge.*

"Fine. Will you please ask *her* to make the call? It can't wait."

Kendra raised her chin. He sounded patronizing, in an overly patient sort of way. Like he was talking to a slow child. But then, maybe she was being too sensitive. She loved having him in her home, but it was weird having him here in *her* workspace, taking over. It was one thing to take orders from him when she arrived at the mission in Idaho last November. That was his team. But Denver was *her* city.

She pursed her lips, and turning out of his office to find Lucinda, she ran straight into their boss, SAC Oxley. "Oh! Excuse me, sir." Her cheeks prickled with heat.

"Agent Dean. Welcome back to work." He shook her hand. "Sanchez got you hopping already?" Oxley chuckled. "He's been a tremendous addition to the Denver team." He patted Rick's shoulder. "Dean, I've assigned you to work his case until you return to the K9 Unit. Stop by my office to get your new weapon issued."

Acid nipped at the lining of Kendra's stomach. "Yes sir. And yes, Agent Sanchez has me hopping. Excuse me." She tossed a glare over her shoulder at the new office golden boy. He scrunched his brows at her in return, as if he had no idea what was wrong with the scenario.

AFTER BRIEFING THE SAC ON THE MOST RECENT MURDER, Rick went to find Kendra. He slid his suit coat on as he left his office and walked down the row of cubicles toward the elevators. As he neared the lobby, a pair of high-heeled, black Betty-Boop platforms intrigued him. Especially since they led his gaze up a pair of alluringly shaped calves that extended out into the walkway from the reception area. The vision was certainly worth investigating. As he approached, his gaze followed the long legs up to the hem of a short black skirt, lush hips, and a trim waist. His perusal rested for a second longer than it should on the snug sweater before he found himself staring at Lucinda's pretty, matte-red smile. She pulled a pen from her long blonde hair which she wore twisted up at the back of her head.

"Well, hello Agent Sanchez." Lucinda's voice was light and airy. "Can I help you with... anything?"

Rick chuckled and leaned forward, his forearms resting on the reception counter. He gave her an equally suggestive grin. "I'm sure you can. But first off, why don't you start calling me Rick."

"All right, *Rick*." Lucinda tucked her heels underneath her seat and rose from her chair to perch on the corner of her desk. She canted her body toward him. A mysterious spicy scent wafted into his nose, something sweet with an undertone of clove. "What else can I do for you?"

A few ideas flickered at the edge of Rick's mind, but he forced his focus back to work. "Did you get ahold of the

Littleton Police Department about maintaining the crime scene until Agent Dean and I get there?"

"Of course, I did." She slid the tip of her tongue across her plump bottom lip. "Anything else?"

He fought the pull of her charms, but indulged in one last inhale of her perfume.

"Excuse me." Kendra's sharp tone snapped him back to the present. "I hope I'm not interrupting anything important, but didn't you say you were in a hurry to get to the crime scene?"

Rick stood up and took a step away from the counter. A sensation resembling guilt washed over him, but he didn't have any reason to feel guilty. There was nothing wrong with him appreciating a beautiful woman, was there? "Yes, let's go."

Kendra gave him a hard stare before she turned toward the bank of elevators. Rick sent Lucinda a quick wink. "Thanks, Lucinda. See you this afternoon."

"I look forward to it. Bye." Lucinda fluttered glossy, red-tipped fingers at him. A soft, appreciative smile curved her lips.

Rick ducked into the elevator behind Kendra just as the doors were closing.

"If you've got better things to do, I can handle the crime scene on my own." Kendra's voice remained hard, and she stared at the lit numbers above the door.

"What's your problem?" He knew, but didn't think it was fair. He was only enjoying what Lucinda put out on a platter.

"Don't tell me you're going to be *that* guy. I had such a better opinion of you."

"What?" Rick waited for Kendra to step out of the compartment before he followed.

"You guys, you're all just putty in her hands. It's pathetic."

He opened the building door for her. "What's with you? Are you jealous?"

Kendra stopped in her tracks and spun to face him. He knew instantly he'd overstepped, but didn't know how to fix it.

"Jealous of what, exactly?"

Rick didn't dare say anything. No words would help him now.

"The last thing I could possibly want is a bunch of idiotic men drooling over my high heels." She glared at him and turned away. "Where's your car?"

Chapter Seven

R ick kept his mouth shut and pointed across the parking garage to his newly assigned Explorer. He started off toward his car, but within twenty feet it occurred to him that Kendra was racing to keep up with his stride, so he shortened his step.

"You doing okay? Are you sure you're ready to be back at work?"

"Of course I'm ready. I'm not sick, I just got bumped on the head." Kendra snapped.

He hadn't meant to insult her. "It would be easier for you if you were sick. A concussion is serious, and I don't want you to push too hard right away. You could relapse, you know."

"I'm fine." She huffed. "I should probably drive. This is my town, and I'm more familiar with the area than you."

Rick clicked the key-fob and the door unlocked. He met Kendra's gaze over the top of the car. "Did I do something to piss you off?"

"No. Why?"

Her face told a different story and Rick decided she'd be

an awful poker player. He shrugged. "You just seem irritated, that's all." He opened his door and slid behind the wheel. "I-70 west to C-470, right?"

Kendra flashed him a heated look out of the corner of her eye. "Yeah. I'll put the exact location in the GPS."

What the hell? Now she's pissed off because I know how to get there? Rick clenched his jaw determined not to let her goad him into a reaction. Maybe mood swings were part of having a head injury. They drove in silence past the Purina factory, through the I-25 exchange, and continued west until they looped onto C-470, southbound. "Which exit am I looking for?" Rick ventured.

"Take Wadsworth, south." Kendra turned her body to face him. "It's just weird having you here. You're brand new in Denver and already taking charge at the office."

Rick glanced at her before returning his gaze to the highway. "It's my case, Kendra. I've been working it for almost a year. Sure as shit, I'm in charge."

She straightened and crossed her arms over her chest. "I don't mean just in charge of the case."

Irritation flicked the muscles at the back of his neck. "What the hell do you mean, then?"

Kendra was silent for a full minute before she answered. "Never mind."

Rick ground his molars together. "Look, I don't know what your problem is, but I need your help on this case. You're the only one who's come in contact with this guy and lived to tell about it."

"But I can't remember anything."

"Not yet, but you might." Rick tapped his thumbs on the steering wheel. "You remembered that the last victim didn't have blood on her clothes when you found her."

"Yeah, so?"

"When the cops got there, the victim had been mutilated

and was covered in blood. The side of her head was smashed with a rock. Those things had to have happened at some point between him knocking you out and the cops' arrival. This guy plans out what he's doing. He has a routine."

"Why would he smash the head of a person who's already dead?"

"I don't know, but I'm gonna figure it out."

"I'm still wondering why he let me live. Maybe he thought I *was* dead?" Kendra sounded more like herself now that she was re-engaging with the case.

"I doubt it. He definitely has a process and we're piecing it together. His victims all have traces of Rohypnol in their systems. They were likely roofied before the guy strangled them. Each time he waits until after the women are dead to crush their skulls and remove their ribs." Rick chewed on his lower lip. "Why the postmortem violence, and why take a rib?"

"Presumably, it's a trophy."

"Right, but why a rib? There has to be a reason. Also, none of the women have been sexually molested. That seems unusual to me. Strangulation is a personal type of murder. He's looking into his victim's face as she takes her last breath."

"Kind of. I mean, her lack of consciousness keeps him distant in a way. What do the profilers say?"

"I've talked to a couple. They all think this guy knows his victims." Rick pulled off at their exit. "Maybe that's why he let you live—because he doesn't know you?"

"Maybe, but didn't you say this string of murders started in Tennessee, and then there were two in Illinois, and another in Kansas?" Kendra swiped the screen on her phone and pulled up a map of the United States. "Do you think he's traveling to women he knows? Or finding women that fit a certain profile along his way?"

"I don't know. So far we can't find anything that connects the victims. Only one of the Illinois women had ever been to Tennessee, and we still haven't found any link between the Tennessee victim and her." Rick turned off the highway and drove to the park entrance.

"So, now we have two more vics, both found southwest of Denver. This afternoon, we can delve into whether or not these two women are connected, and if so, how."

"This is the first time he's murdered twice in the same city." They pulled up behind a Douglas County Sheriff's vehicle. "There's got to be a reason why."

Kendra pushed to keep up with Rick's long-legged stride as he approached the junior officer in charge of securing the crime scene. He showed his badge and signed the list of investigators visiting the scene before ducking under the yellow tape. Kendra did the same, then pulled out a pair of rubber gloves. She snapped several pictures of the general area with her phone before she caught up to Rick. The nauseating decaying fruit scent of death lay heavy in the morning air.

The body of a young woman in her late teens or twenties, lay on her back with her ankles crossed and her hands positioned together over her chest. Her eyes bulged open and dark purple and blue finger marks streaked across her neck. Dried blood caked her hair and stained a jagged tear in her blouse where her lower left rib had been removed. Kendra's vision clouded with a kaleidoscope of lights and colors. She grabbed Rick's arm to stabilize herself so she wouldn't fall and choked on the sudden acidic bile burning her throat.

"Dean? You okay?" Rick grasped her shoulders and guided

her to a large rock on the side of the path. "Sit down. Put your head between your knees."

"I'm fine." She shook him off.

"Like hell. You shouldn't be out here. You're not ready."

Rick's mothering rubbed raw against her nerves. "I told you, I am fine." She glared up at him. "It's just that he lay this woman out in the exact manner as the one I came across. The only difference is the blood and rib."

"Yeah. We're pretty sure, in your situation, he was coming back for the dead woman's rib when he found you there."

"So... he doesn't take the bones at the time of the murder? Or, maybe he just didn't have the right tools with him when he killed the woman I discovered on my path. What does the ME say about the timing of the rib removal?"

"Only that it's postmortem and probably snapped off with a bolt cutter. It's a good question though. This asshole may murder emotionally, but removes his trophy later for a different reason, for some twisted purpose of his own."

Kendra rubbed the back of her neck. "Has a K-9 team been here yet? Maybe they can discover where the guy came from, or went to after he finished." Kendra swallowed hard against the sudden lump in her throat. She attempted to cover her emotion by taking more photos. "We're about a quarter mile from the parking area. That's a long way to haul a body. Any signs of a struggle? Or drag marks?"

One of the crime scene investigators answered. "No signs of struggle. Not even on the ground where she lays."

Rick braced his hands on his hips. "If she were already dead, it fits our guy's MO." He stared Kendra in the eye. "Of course, we'll get the official report from the ME, but it's looking like he drugs the women and strangles them somewhere else. Then he hauls them out to the wilderness, hits them in the head with a rock, removes a rib, and then poses them." He cast his gaze to the sky. "It's a lot of steps. Why?"

"All the victims were found in the wilderness?"

Rick nodded and turned to take in the surroundings. "Do you think that means something?"

Kendra stood and joined Rick. "Everything might mean something."

Chapter Eight

❦

Abbot Lee lay prone, the sun hot on his back causing the fresh wounds from his recent ascetic cleanse to throb with the righteousness they helped procure. Clean, pure air filled his lungs. He shifted his weight and raised his elbow off the ground, brushing several hard pieces of gravel that stuck to his skin away with his other hand.

The view through the binoculars was clear from his perch at the top of the ridge where he'd been watching the scene below for over two hours. An investigative team swarmed the area where he had left the guilty woman. They were like bees around a hive. That dark soul received what she deserved— no more, no less. Sinful women must be shunned—sent out from society and stoned to death. It was the law. He knew because Daddy made him memorize it.

"This is the law of jealousy: when a wife, being under the authority of her husband, goes astray and defiles herself, or when a spirit of jealousy comes over a man and he is jealous of his wife, he shall then make the woman stand before the Lord, and shall apply all the law to her. Moreover, the man will be free from guilt, but that woman shall bear hers."

Abbot closed his eyes and briefly wandered through the images of his childhood. His daddy... the brutal vengeance Daddy visited upon his mother... and why. He squeezed his lids tight before opening them again. The memories still cut deep, even though he knew Daddy was only obeying the law. The woman who gave birth to him was a dirty whore. Daddy said so.

Gratified that he was able to remove another devil's harlot from the world, Abbot prepared to return to his van. He reached for the worn leather case, but in the second before he slid the binoculars away from his face, he caught a glimpse of a black SUV pulling into the roped-off parking area. Abbot settled back into his position to observe the new arrival.

A tall, dark man in an expensive-looking suit, unfolded his frame from the driver's side. He slid reflective sunglasses over his eyes. The passenger-side door opened, and a woman stepped out. The two walked side by side to the police sentry. *There are already detectives down there, so who are these people?* He smoothed the dirt under his elbows and propped the lenses against his cheeks to observe.

The woman... she seemed familiar, but he didn't know her. He couldn't place her. The couple ducked under the yellow tape and walked together toward the scene of his act of redemption. *When they see the body, they'll understand.* The woman and the suit approached a group of other investigators and she turned briefly to the side, pushing her hair over her shoulder. He saw her face full on. She wore a wide bandage on her forehead. And he remembered.

Cold needles of shock spiked through his skull. *It's her! She's following me. How'd she find me? How could she know?* He sat up, gulping air. Drops of sweat popped out along his hairline and his heart rapped a demanding cadence against his ribcage. He wiped his eyes and stared through the lenses once again. *It is her—without a doubt. Does she know about my penance?*

What does she want from me? I thought she was innocent, but she's no better than the others. Look how she teases me with her long hair and... His gaze panned her figure. His body stiffened. Desire blossomed. *I should have killed her when I had the chance. She was lying right there for me. A gift from God, and I was too soft—too stupid to realize it. That fucking dog tried to attack me and I lost my focus. Daddy would be so disappointed.*

He muttered another verse under his breath. *"With her many persuasions she entices him; With her flattering lips she seduces him. Suddenly he follows her as an ox goes to the slaughter, or as one in fetters to the discipline of a fool. Until an arrow pierces through his liver; as a bird hastens to the snare, so he does not know that it will cost him his life. Now therefore, my sons, listen to me, and pay attention to the words of my mouth. Do not let your heart turn aside to her ways, do not stray into her paths. For many are the victims she has cast down, and numerous are all her slain. Her house is the way to Sheol, descending to the chambers of death."*

He was no longer safe. That witch-woman could probably sense his presence. A speedy escape was his only option. He packed up his gear and scrambled for cover in the trees. *I'll find out who she is and get to her before she gets to me. If she wants me, she'll have me, only on my terms.* His sour breath came fast. The sun rose in the sky and pressed fiery fingers against his neck and shoulders as he ran through the woods to his van.

The dented door groaned when he wrenched it open. Abbot clambered into the driver's seat and slammed the door shut. He turned the key in the ignition, but it merely clicked. His pulse kicked up another level and his head swam. With a deep breath, he attempted to calm himself and rotated the key a second time. Still nothing. His heart burst into his throat.

He threw open the hood and wiggled a few wires. White crumbling corrosion covered the battery connectors. "Damnation!" Abbot bustled to the cab and rummaged under the seat for something hard and heavy. He found a bolt-cutter and used it to pound on the corroded bolts.

He ran to the van and tried the ignition again. The roar of the engine soothed the prickles bumping across the surface of his skin. He slammed the hood and once back inside, yanked on the gear lever. The van lurched forward and bounced down the two-track path until it joined the C-470 frontage road. One more mile and he would be on the highway and free.

Free to cleanse himself again before figuring out who that devious woman was and coming up with a plan to catch her unaware.

Chapter Nine

gent Burke Cameron had only been in the FBI one year and was excited to be part of a team that was hunting a serial killer. This was the big leagues, and it gave him a chance to prove himself. He parked his car in front of a small bungalow in Washington Park, home to the husband of the victim Kendra found. He took a deep breath and let it out slow.

"This is it." He said to his partner riding shot-gun.

Agent Stott gripped the door handle. "I hate this part of the job. This murder has just ruined all these people's lives, and now we have to poke the sore."

"Yeah, but they might know something that helps us find a killer. Let's go." Burke wasn't eager to disturb the family either, but it was a necessary means of gathering information. You never knew. Family members, especially spouses, were often guilty of murders. Of course, that was less likely in a serial killer case that spanned several states. Burke's fingertips grazed the cold butt of his weapon—an automatic check.

The duo approached the house. A black shaggy dog barked at them from the side yard and slow, heavy footsteps sounded from inside. A man in his mid-thirties opened the door.

"Mr. Kaufman?"

"Yes." The man blinked at the offending sunlight.

"We're Agents Cameron and Stott from the FBI. We'd like to ask you a few questions about your wife, if you don't mind."

Mr. Kaufman hesitated and a bewildered expression crossed his features.

"We'll only take a few minutes of your time." Burke reached forward and touched the man's shoulder. "I know this is difficult, but we want to do everything we can to find your wife's murderer."

The man nodded absently and trudged back into the house, leaving the agents to follow him if they chose to. They did. Drawn curtains kept the front room dark and musty. A plate of dried-up, half-eaten food sat off kilter, teetering from a stack of magazines on the coffee table. Voices from an infomercial droned on, but Mr. Kaufman had the volume turned down too low to make out the words.

Burke waited until the man slid back into his chair. "We're sorry to intrude on your grief, Mr. Kaufman, but can you tell us about the day you last saw your wife?"

The man's sorrow-worn eyes panned toward Burke. He didn't speak right away and when he did, his voice sounded rusty. "I saw her last that morning, before I left for work."

"Did she tell you her plans for that day? Do you know if she was meeting anyone?"

Mr. Kaufman's eyes stared off at a mystery point some-where beyond Burke's shoulder and slowly filled with tears. His head swung to one side, and then the other, a choking sound barked from this throat. "No," he cried. "I didn't give her the chance."

"What do you mean?" Burke perched on the edge of this

chair and leaned forward, bracing himself on his knee. "What happened that morning?"

Mr. Kaufman's gaze swam to meet Burke's. "We fought." He rubbed a fist across his tears. "I was pre-occupied with work. Lisa tried to tell me about something, but I wasn't listening." He dissolved into tears. "Now I'll never hear her voice again."

Burke ground his teeth together, fighting back his own sympathy. "We're doing all we can to find out who killed your wife." He yanked a tissue from its box on the table and thrust it at the grieving man. Rocked by the man's sobs, Burke regretted being so gung-ho about interviewing him. He pulled in a breath through his mouth. "Is there anything you can remember? Did Lisa meet anyone new lately? Did she say she was going out?"

The man wiped his eyes and nose, then cleared his throat. Agent Stott who had been standing near the door stepped forward. "Would you like a glass of water, Mr. Kaufman? Or a whiskey, maybe?"

A hint of a smile crossed Mr. Kaufman's mouth. "Whiskey would be good. There's some on the sideboard in the dining room." He blew his nose. "Help yourselves, too."

Burke offered a slight smile. "Can't while we're on duty, but thank you."

Drier eyes sought his. "You know, maybe Lisa *did* say something about going out. She planned to go shopping, I think. She said something about 16th Street." He ran a hand over his face. "God, I can't remember. I didn't really care." Tears flowed fresh. "I'd give anything to have another chance to care."

"Anything you can remember might be of help. For now, let us get you some food to eat with your drink." Burke nodded to Stott who turned into the kitchen.

The man searched Burke's face. "They told me the

murderer maimed her body in some way. Why?" Another sob escaped and fresh tears flooded his bloodshot eyes. "Why would someone do that?"

Burke shook his head, silently wondering if the ME or anyone else told him that they found his wife's wedding ring shoved down her throat. "How were things between the two of you?" He swallowed. "It sounds like maybe you were a little distant with each other. I hate to ask this, but could there have been another man?"

"Oh, God," Mr. Kaufman cried. "I don't think so, but—," he broke down.

Burke placed a reassuring hand on the man's shoulder. "I'm sorry for your grief, and I wish we didn't have to ask these hard questions."

Pain-filled eyes looked up at him. "No, I'm sorry I wasn't a better husband."

Pressing his lips together, Burke reached into his inside coat pocket and pulled out a card. "Here's my contact information. If you remember something, or think of anything else at all, even if it doesn't seem important to you, I want you to call me. Okay?"

Mr. Kaufman nodded and accepted a plate of re-heated casserole from Agent Stott, freshening the room with the aroma of melted cheese and tomato sauce—most likely a selection from one of the many dishes stuffed in the refrigerator brought over by friends and family. Burke stood and shook Mr. Kaufman's hand.

"We'll be in touch."

"Thank you." Kaufman's eyes hardened. "Find him, Agent Cameron. Find the bastard who killed my Lisa."

"We'll do our best." Burke and his partner left the small house, closing the door behind them. Silent in thought, they made their way to the car. As he shut his car door, Burke heard his name shouted across the lawn.

"Agent Cameron!" Mr. Kaufman ran out across the lawn, barefoot and in flannel pants. "Wait! I think I remembered something."

Burke stepped back out of the car and inclined his head to listen.

"She *was* going to shop downtown, but changed her mind. I remember her saying she wanted to drive out to Park Meadows Mall instead."

"Okay, good. That helps, Mr. Kaufman." Burke pursed his lips. That meant the woman's abduction likely happened south of Denver, closer to where they found her body.

Chapter Ten

U p with the sun, Kendra bathed Baxter and when he was dry, she buckled on his best collar and badge holder. She dressed in a dark navy pant-suit for the special occasion. A touch of oil slicked back her long hair that she rolled and pinned in a tight, regulation bun at her nape.

"Ready to go? It's your big day." Kendra helped Baxter climb into the back of her Jeep.

When they arrived at the auditorium inside the FBI building, a support staffer escorted Kendra and Baxter to a room behind the stage to wait for the ceremony to begin. Also in the room were the Director of the Denver FBI, the Deputy Director and her direct K9 supervisor, Clay Jennings with his K9, Gunner.

The directors greeted Kendra and patted Baxter's head. Clay hugged her while Baxter and Gunner sniffed each other to get reacquainted. At nine o'clock a.m., a voice sounded over the speaker asking the room to come to order. An admin escorted the group to the wings of the stage and directed them to a line of seats behind the podium.

After sitting, Kendra looked out at the full room mostly

filled with other FBI agents, but also in attendance were several K9 Police Officers she and Baxter had worked with and come to know over the years. She noticed some fire fighters and first responders she'd met along the way. It reminded her that all the careers represented here were in the name of keeping the public safe. And all these people were here to honor Baxter. A warm pride puffed her chest, and she ran her fingers over Baxter's long floppy ear.

Kendra searched for the team she was currently assigned to, and found them sitting together on the right side, middle. Rick nodded and Burke raised a hand to wave. She smiled, slightly uncomfortable to be at the center of such a presti-gious award ceremony.

The master of ceremonies began the program "Good morning and thank you all for coming to honor one of our own this morning. Please stand for the Pledge of Allegiance." When Kendra and Clay stood for the pledge, so did their K9 partners.

The speaker continued, "We are here today to honor K9 Baxter who is receiving the Federal Bureau of Investigation Medal of Valor. We present the FBI Medal of Valor in recog-nition of an exceptional act of heroism or voluntary risk of personal safety and life. This act must have occurred in the direct line of duty or within the scope of FBI employment and in the face of criminal adversaries."

The announcer held out her hand and Kendra stood with Baxter and approached the podium. Kendra reached down to slip off Baxter's collar and handed it to Clay. Her eyes pricked and she ground her teeth together and pinched the inside of one hand to keep from embarrassing herself in front of all her fellow agents and officers.

"Special Agent Kendra Dean was rendered unconscious and her K9 partner, Baxter, attacked the fugitive who struck her. K9 Baxter is a sniffer dog, but he stepped into the role of biter to protect the life of his partner and fellow agent. Technically, this medal is awarded only for injury incurred during the call of duty, but we granted an exception for K9 Baxter because our dogs do not work on a time clock. They are always on duty." The woman opened a flat square box. She lifted a blue satin ribbon holding a golden shield medallion and handed it to Kendra who raised it for the crowd to see. Applause erupted with a simultaneous standing ovation.

That was it. By the time Kendra slid the ribbon over Baxter's head and the medal gleamed at his chest, she was fully crying with tears and mascara all over her cheeks. She faced Baxter and stood at attention. The crowd went silent and Kendra saluted her life-saving hero and partner, K9 Baxter. Applause exploded once again.

The woman leaned toward the microphone and continued. "We would like to congratulate K9 Baxter on a brave and successful career as a K9 FBI Agent. In his career he found many lost children and people in distress. Prevented bombing attacks and assisted in countless multi-state drug arrests. Last year he located a federal agent lost in a blizzard in Idaho. This month, Baxter saved the life of his partner and sacrificed his leg performing his duty with bravery, valor, loyalty, and love.

To this end, we wish K9 Baxter a peaceful and enjoyable retirement living with his new owner, Special Agent Dean."

Kendra turned to the master of ceremonies. She pulled a crisp one-dollar bill from her inside coat pocket and presented it to the woman who accepted it in exchange for a manila envelope.

The crowd rushed to its feet a final time. The people on the stage with Kendra gathered around Baxter and her offering congratulations. Mortified by her lack of emotional control, Kendra broke down. Clay grabbed her by the shoulders and with a broad smile, drew Kendra into his arms.

"Go ahead and cry. You're not the only one here in tears. Besides, any one of us on the K9 team would do the same if it were our own partners."

Kendra nodded into his shoulder, knowing that she was wiping makeup all over his suit. She felt Clay pull back, and she looked up.

"I think there's some people who want to talk to you."

Kendra turned around and smiled a soggy smile at Agents Sanchez and Cameron. Burke grinned and crouched down to look at Baxter's medal. Rick's eyes were overflowing with what she interpreted as compassion or maybe something deeper.

"Hey, congratulations, to both Baxter and you." Rick held out his hand as though to shake hers, but when she reached for it, he pulled her toward him and embraced her. "I'm so proud of you, Kendra."

"It was all Baxter."

Rick held her shoulders and leaned back to look into her eyes. "A team is never singular. This was an honoring ceremony—very moving." His gaze moved to something behind her, and Kendra felt him shift as one of his hands left her arm. "I'm Rick Sanchez."

Kendra pivoted to see who Rick was talking to.

The men shook hands. "Clay Jennings—K9, good to meet you."

Rick nodded, assessing Clay. "You two work together?"

Kendra jumped in. "Yes, Agent Jennings is my boss."

"You're a lucky man," Rick didn't immediately release Clay's hand.

Clay narrowed his eyes, and it seemed to Kendra that an entire silent conversation happened above her head. "Yes, I am. So are you, it seems—with Agent Dean assigned to your team for the time being." Clay dropped his gaze to Kendra and his smile softened. "I hope you'll be coming back to us soon."

"I do too." Uncomfortable with the awkward tension she patted Baxter's head. "But for now, let's go get cake."

In the refreshment line, Rick asked, "What was the significance of the dollar for the envelope part of the ceremony?"

Kendra smiled. "Technically, the dogs belong to the United States Government, so when they retire or can no longer work, if their partner wants to adopt them they have to purchase them. Even though these dogs are worth tens of thousands of dollars, the purchase is somewhat token, but paying a dollar makes it legal. The envelope contains his papers."

"That's cool."

"Yeah, it is." Kendra lifted a slice of cake onto her plate and licked a dollop of buttercream frosting from her finger. She cocked her head and leveled her gaze on Rick. "What was the significance of that weirdness between you and Clay?"

"Heh. Nothing for you to worry about. We were just settling a few things."

Kendra rolled her eyes. "Men are so weird."

Chapter Eleven

F or breakfast on Saturday morning, Kendra set up Baxter's new bowl stand that elevated his food and water so he wouldn't have to balance bending forward to eat from the floor level. His appetite seemed normal, and as he crunched his kibble, Kendra's shoulders relaxed a little. Baxter adapted much quicker than she did.

After he ate, Kendra took him outside to practice the exercises the vet recommended to help him build the strength he would need to live as a tri-pawed, and then they went on a short walk before lunch. Baxter's gait was already getting smoother as he learned to shift his weight back to his haunches before lifting his solo front leg to hop forward.

While Baxter napped, Kendra leaned against the kitchen counter and googled local lakes where she could take him to swim. The vet told her that was one of the best exercises for dogs with an amputation. Normally, she would have taken him to Chatfield Reservoir since it was the closest, but after finding the recent murder victim there, the idea ran cold. Instead, Kendra found a dog park close to the reservoir entrance.

"Come on, Bax. Let's get you some social time." Kendra unhooked his lead from its peg in the closet and Baxter sat at her feet wagging his tail. "Ready for some fun, are you? Okay, Buddy, let's go." She attached his leash and led him to her Jeep.

Kendra parked next to a white van that had seen better days and helped Baxter get out of the car. She walked him to the gate of the dog-park open space. Once inside, she unclipped him, and he teetered off to greet other dogs. A Saint Bernard bounded across the dried weeds straight for Baxter and Kendra held her breath. Baxter attempted to brace up, but he tumbled. The larger animal, thinking this was a form of play pounced on him and Kendra's chest squeezed tight. She ran toward her dog.

"Baxter!"

Before she could get there, Baxter rolled over and sprang back up, barking and wagging his tail. Kendra stopped and watched, her heart thudding, the ever-present protective-encrusted guilt thickening her throat as the dogs ran off to the far edge of the park together.

"What happened to your dog?" A male voice sounded from behind her.

Startled, Kendra turned and glared up at a tall, gangly man. "Is that your Saint Bernard?"

"Nope." He squinted at her and tossed long mousy bangs out of his pale hazel eyes. "But it looks like he's just a big teddy bear. Doesn't seem to realize how big he is, but it don't look like he's hurting your dog." The man crossed his arms as he watched the animals play. "That dog of yours seems to get around pretty well. What happened to his leg?"

"Someone shot him."

Kendra's bald statement had the desired effect. The man drew his chin back and stared at her. Relieved from engaging in inane social banter, she made her way to a bench.

It looked as though the guy was going to follow her, but when her phone chimed, he turned and went the other way.

"Hello?"

"Hey, where are you?" Rick's deep voice vibrated through the speaker and eased her agitation.

"At the dog park with Baxter, why?"

"I'm at your house. I stopped by to see how Baxter was doing."

"Stopped by? Isn't your apartment in Lowry? That's almost an hour's drive."

Rick chuckled. "Yeah, well, I also wanted to talk to you. I'm still hoping you've remembered more from the day you got hit in the head?"

"Not really. I've been busy with Baxter." Kendra had a few fuzzy dreams about that afternoon, but no definitive memories formed in her brain. "I don't think I saw the guy. I have a clear memory of the branch coming at me right before it crashed into my head, but nothing else solid. A few sounds... maybe his voice, but nothing I'm absolutely certain of."

"Well, that's more than you remembered before. That's a good sign. Where's the dog park?" Rick's tone deepened slightly. "Mind if I come hang out with you there?"

Tiny bubbles raced through Kendra's body. She glanced down at her jeans with the holes in the knees and ran her fingers over her hair which she had pulled into a sloppy ponytail and grimaced. "I guess." She looked about as polar opposite to Lucinda as she possibly could. *Damn.*

Kendra gave him directions to the park. After she slid her phone back into her pocket, she yanked out her hairband and combed through the tangles with her fingers. She'd never given a single hoot about what her other co-workers thought of her appearance, but with Rick it was different. *He doesn't care, and neither should I*, she told herself even as she fished a lip-gloss out of her bag.

Fifteen minutes later Rick's SUV pull into the lot. He stepped out in dark blue Levi's and a snug fitting V-neck t-shirt. The sun glinted off his sunglasses as he searched for her. She stood and waved. The bright smile he flashed at her when he saw her made her knees quiver. *Does he always have to look so good?* Kendra tugged at her own faded sweatshirt.

"Hey." His voice smoothed over her skin like warm whiskey and she fought not to do something stupid like bat her eyelashes.

She smiled. "Hi."

"How's our boy doing?"

Our boy? Kendra gripped the back of the bench wondering why such an innocent phrase caused her to heat up. "He seems to be having a good time—as though he's forgotten he ever had four legs."

Rick dug into a plastic grocery bag and pulled out two bottles of iced tea. He handed her one. "Thought you might be thirsty."

"Thanks." She reached for the bottle and her fingers closed over his. Her gaze flew to his face. It was as if the oxygen was sucked out of the air. For a brief second, Kendra didn't breathe. It unnerved her that she couldn't see Rick's eyes clearly enough to read his emotions behind his dark lenses. She looked away—at her feet, at the bench, then searching for Baxter. "There he is." She pointed, hoping Rick couldn't detect the bumping of her pulse in her voice.

"Looks like he's doing great." Rick snapped the lid on his drink and took a long swig. "How about you? Anymore headaches or anything?"

"No. No more headaches, but I am having crazy dreams."

Rick touched her elbow, pressing her toward the bench causing the nerve endings in her skin to spike. "You should sit down." He sat next to her, their thighs only a whisper apart.

"Are your dreams about being attacked? Do you think you're remembering more?"

"I don't know, I don't think so." She watched Baxter wobble around sniffing other dogs. "I'm sorry."

Rick set his palm on her knee and squeezed leaving a hot imprint and setting her heart off again. "You have nothing to be sorry about. I'm just grasping at straws." He took his hand back and adjusted his seat several inches away from her. Kendra stared at him, marveling at her sudden sense of loss.

WHAT AM I DOING HERE? RICK ONLY MEANT TO ENCOURAGE her, but he immediately found out that touching Kendra was a risky prospect. The simple act of resting his palm on her leg sent a battalion of fiery impulses throughout his system. He had pulled his hand away from her and the look she gave him seemed confused. He cursed himself. Kendra wasn't just some chick at a bar. Someone to take home when the pub closed down, tumble in the sheets with, and then never see again. His body responded to her in a dangerous way. Rick knew he had to watch it. He'd made himself a promise, and he intended to keep it.

With a long swig of bitter tea, Rick reminded himself that Kendra deserved a man who could care for her. One who could love her. No matter how wonderful it felt to be near her, he wasn't that guy. That part of his heart was dead. It died on March 28th in Chicago, three years ago, and his hormones needed to remember that.

Chapter Twelve

Rick arrived at the headquarters building early. He hadn't slept well. Strange, emotional nightmares and flashbacks had him tossing and turning. So he rolled out of bed and got ready for work. Rick liked to be the only one in the office first thing in the morning. He concentrated best in the silence before the rest of the team showed up.

On the elevator up to his floor, Rick read through Cameron and Stott's interview report. The only useful piece of information they gleaned from Mr. Kaufman was that he thought his wife might have been shopping at the Park Meadows Mall, located south of Denver. That made sense location wise. If she was abducted at the mall or somewhere nearby, it wasn't very far from there to where her body was discovered.

The one out-of-place factor was that this had been a second murder in the same city. This killer had never done that before. If it weren't for the head trauma, the missing rib, and the wedding ring, Rick would question if it were the same guy at all. But the inclusion of those two crucial factors meant it had to be him.

The elevator doors slid open, and he stepped out onto the third floor, his eyes still riveted to the file.

Her spicy scent enveloped him before he saw her. "Good morning, Rick."

He glanced up and was rewarded with a full-length view of the lovely Lucinda. Today she swathed her perfect figure in a purple silk, wrap-around dress. She wore part of her hair down in long luscious waves with the rest knotted on top of her head.

"Good morning." Rick failed to keep his eyes on her face. "You're here early."

"So are you." A soft laugh floated from her mouth. "No one else will be here for at least another hour."

Rick's eyes snapped up to gauge her expression. Did he imagine the suggestive tone in her voice, or was she actually hinting at something? Lucinda turned toward the break room before he could judge and afforded him a bewitching view of her hips swaying underneath the soft fabric. His gaze traveled down her legs to the spiked purple heels that matched her dress.

He shook his head and smiled to himself. *That woman is trouble.* He strode down the hall to his office and buried himself in the case. An insistent gnawing in his belly reminded him he had eaten nothing for breakfast. He glanced up when the scent of freshly brewed coffee infused the air.

"Thought you might like a cup." Lucinda, holding a steaming cup of java, leaned against the doorframe.

"Thanks. You must have read my mind. Do you know if there's any food in the kitchen? Even just a granola bar would do. I'm suddenly starving."

Lucinda brought the coffee to him and bent to set it on

his desk. She strategically aimed her cleavage in his direction. "What are you hungry for?" She looked into his eyes.

Rick pushed his chair back. If this were any place else besides his office, he'd pick up what she was laying down. "I'm not particular."

"I can order something for delivery if you like. Maybe bagels or a breakfast sandwich?" She sat back against his desk. "We definitely want you to keep your energy up."

He laughed, unable to pretend like he didn't know what she was up to. "That'd be great. Why don't you order a couple dozen? My team will be here soon."

She smirked at him and slid off the desk toward the door. She glanced over her shoulder. "Let me know if you want anything else."

"I will." Rick watched her walk away and then got to work.

Breakfast arrived and Lucinda brought him a toasted onion-bagel, with egg, and cheese and a fresh cup of coffee. "Here we are."

"That smells like heaven. Thanks, Lucinda." Rick unwrapped his sandwich and took too big of a bite. His hunger welled up, and he leaned back in his chair to enjoy the satisfying meal.

Lucinda laughed a delicate tinkle of a sound and lifted a napkin to the corner of his mouth. "You are a hungry boy, aren't you?"

"He looks like he's practically starving to death." Kendra's sarcastic tone sent ice crystals through his veins.

Rick sat up with a jolt, coming face to face, an inch from Lucinda. She wore a satisfied feline smirk on her pink lips. That felt too close, so he stood and pushed his chair back. "Ken—Agent Dean, I'm glad you're here. Is Cameron here yet?"

Her eyes narrowed slightly as she studied Rick. For the

life of him, he didn't know why he was acting like he was guilty of something. He hadn't done or said anything inappropriate. It wasn't his fault that Lucinda was an incorrigible flirt.

Kendra pointed to the side of her mouth and tapped the skin. "You still have a little egg on your face... Lucinda, you have the napkin. Why don't you finish... whatever you two were doing? I'll be at my desk." She walked away and looked at him over her shoulder. "I'll let Cameron know you're looking for him." She spun around, her ponytail swinging in the air.

Shit. Rick stared at Kendra's back as she made her way to her cubicle.

Lucinda moved to wipe his cheek, and he snatched the napkin from her. "I got it." Rick turned his back to her and stalked to the window, glowering at the view. He propped his hands on his hips and released a sigh. It pissed him off that Kendra elicited such a response in him. He didn't owe her anything. He had done nothing wrong. *What the hell?*

SO, RICK SANCHEZ WAS THAT KIND OF GUY. SHE SHOULD have known. He was too good looking. Too confident. Good thing she found out about him now, before she let herself really start to care. Kendra admitted to herself that she was attracted to Rick. What red-blooded woman wouldn't be? She had thought there might be something between them, but now she knew he probably made all women feel like that. What with that drop-dead grin and his smoldering obsidian eyes. Kendra shivered in spite of herself.

She looked down at her no-nonsense twill slacks, work shirt, and hiking shoes. There was a figure under there somewhere, she just wasn't advertising. Her face was scrubbed clean of makeup and she'd simply pulled her hair back in an elastic band. No way in hell she could compete with Lucinda's full court press. A gritty surge of anger bubbled up her throat at the thought, and she threw her purse under her desk. *Why the hell would I want to compete with her, anyway?*

Burke's voice teased from behind her. "What'd that purse ever do to you?"

Kendra sent him a rueful look and dropped into her chair. "You're late. The boss is looking for you."

"Is he pissed? Did he yell at you? Is that what's going on?"

Her shoulders sagged. "No. He just wants to see you when you get here. I think he was reading your report. Probably just has a few questions."

"Okay, well, if you need me to kick that purse's ass for you later, just let me know." He winked.

She sent him a self-deprecating smile. "Get out of here."

Burke raised his hands in surrender. "I'm going, no need to get physical."

"Shut-up." Kendra wadded up a piece of paper and threw it at Burke's back as he walked toward Rick's office.

Chapter Thirteen

Rick paced the length of the conference room with his eyes fixed on the wall of evidence in the serial murder case. When Kendra pushed through the door, he had to fight to focus his attention on the facts at hand. To her credit, Kendra maintained a professional attitude. He knew he'd been giving her mixed messages, but it seemed she was content to keep her distance. In the end, that was the best plan. No one would ever break into the cage he'd constructed around his heart.

He thought of the disappointment he saw in her expression at the dog park last weekend when he pulled back from her. God, it would be so easy to indulge in the comfort of those dark chocolate eyes, but they had both come to the unspoken understanding that moving in that direction was not a good idea.

Kendra glanced at him, a wisp of a smile crossing the mouth that showed up frequently in his dreams. He nodded and buried his gaze in the file folder he carried.

"Anything new?" She addressed the room.

Burke gestured to her to come over to his end of the table

so he could show her the photos of all the victims, side by side. "Nothing new. I hate thinking we have to wait around for this asshole to kill again before we can catch him."

"Let's hope not. Keep digging." Kendra picked up a report and leaned back against the table while she read it.

Burke said something too soft for Rick to hear and Kendra laughed, pushing his shoulder playfully. Rick flexed his jaw. Closing his eyes, he reprimanded himself for the surge of inappropriate envy stuffing his chest.

Kendra stood and placed the file back on the stack of evidence reports. "I stopped in to see if any of you guys want me to pick something up for you when I go out for lunch?"

"Where are you going?" Burke reached for his wallet.

"Panera."

"Mind making a stop at McDonalds? I can write you a list."

Kendra laughed. "Why don't you just come with me?"

Burke raised his brows at Rick in question. God, he wanted to say no—to tell Burke that there was too much work—that he couldn't go to lunch, or dinner, or anywhere at all with Kendra. He snatched up his coffee cup, slopping some on the table, and took a gulp. The hot liquid burned his tongue. *Shit.*

Rick swallowed hard. "Yeah, go ahead. We'll rehash all of this one more time after you guys get back." His voice sounded choked and stiff to his own ears.

Kendra focused on him for a few seconds too long. "Can we get you anything?" Her tone soft, like she was talking to a child.

Rick met her gaze but he couldn't hold it and instead shifted his focus to the papers on the table. There were emotions swimming in the depth of her eyes he couldn't—or at least didn't want—to read. Ever since he'd kissed her cheek, there had been some silent communication going on between them. And he did his damnedest to pretend he didn't see it.

"No, thanks. I'll just get something at the cafeteria."

Burke stared at Rick for a second before his gaze drifted to Kendra and then back. He smirked, and Rick wanted to wipe the smug, knowing expression right off his face.

"Hurry up. We have work to do. I want to get this guy before he strikes again."

Burke stood, pulled his suit coat from his chair and slid into it. "Yes, sir. Come on, Ken." He took her arm and they walked to the door. Just as it closed behind them, Kendra glanced back over her shoulder meeting Rick's following gaze with a look of pity. She may as well have slugged him right in the gut.

———

THE TEAM TRIED MANY DIFFERENT THEORIES OUT ON EACH other, re-hashed interviews and evidence until the sun caressed the horizon. At the end of the day, they were no closer to finding the killer than they had been that morning.

Rick ran a hand over his face. "Let's call it a night. You all have put in a solid day. Go home." He stretched his neck side to side.

"Don't have to tell me twice." Burke stood and stacked the papers in front of him. "Anyone want to grab a drink?" Two other agents agreed to meet at the Irish pub down the street. "Sanchez? How about you?"

A beer sounded like the perfect way to release some tension right then. "Yeah, sure. First round's on me."

"Yes! You are my kind of boss." Burke grinned. "Kendra? You coming?"

Her eyes found Rick's and held a question. Rick shrugged

trying to communicate complete indifference. "Yeah, you coming?"

Her smile dazzled him and his blood quickened. "Sure, since *you're* buying." Her laugh was velvet.

Suddenly, Rick wanted her to go with them to the bar more than anything. Well, maybe equally as much as he didn't want the other guys to go anymore. He waited in his office until everyone in the team left for the pub. Not wanting to appear too anxious, he checked his email and scanned his other social media.

"I hear some of the gang went to the pub for happy hour?" Lucinda peeked her head through the door.

Rick glanced her way. "Yeah. They went to Murphy's. Are you going?"

"Are you inviting me?"

She was relentless, but made a beautiful diversion. He grinned. "Sounds like I am."

Her smile was radiant. "I'll wait. We can walk over together."

"Sounds good. I'm almost done."

THURSDAY NIGHT BASEBALL WAS FLASHING FROM THE TV screens around the bar—Rockies vs the Dodgers—but loud pop music drowned out the announcers. The wait staff carried sizzling appetizers to waiting customers, and the savory scents wafting through the air had Rick's stomach growling. The after-work crowd filled the place—lots of people unwinding and loosening up.

Lucinda gripped onto Rick's coat sleeve so they wouldn't get separated on their way to their co-workers' tables. In the bustle, Rick jostled against Kendra's back and she turned to see who bumped her.

"Oh, hi." She looked up at him. "Pretty crowded tonight, isn't it?"

Rick, temporarily lost in her eyes, mumbled some sound. Hopefully, it came across as a yes, or uh-huh.

Her gaze moved from his to Lucinda at his elbow. Her lips flattened into a line and she angled back to the bar.

Sidling up next to her, Rick held his credit card up to get the bartender's attention. He told the guy to put his team's drinks on his tab, and pointed out the tables where everyone was sitting. "And these two ladies' drinks as well." He leaned toward Lucinda. "Why don't you go find a seat with the team? We'll be over in few minutes."

Lucinda smiled up at Rick but the look she sent Kendra's direction held spears of ice.

Kendra's brows quirked, and she gave him a sardonic grin. "You know, Rick, I'm not sure what's going on between you and Lucinda, or between you and me for that matter, but I think we should figure it out. Get it all out in the open, don't you?"

Taken aback by her straightforwardness, Rick rocked onto his heels. "What do you mean?" He tried to buy himself some time.

She gave her head a small shake. "You know exactly what I mean." Her gaze held him in place though his inner voice yelled for him to turn around and run. His physical urging was louder and stronger, and that was the side that won out. He answered her with a slow smile, his gaze dipping to her mouth.

Kendra curled her lips into a soft smile. "Want to go somewhere else where we can talk? Dinner maybe?"

Rick glanced across the room at the other agents drinking and laughing. "I'm supposed to be footing the bill."

"Only for the first round. Don't let these jerks take you for more than that. They'll drink you dry if you let them."

"It's not that."

"Oh. Right. You're here with Lucinda."

"No, I'm not. We only walked over here together."

"Does she know that?" They both looked over at the members of their team. Lucinda waved and pointed to an empty chair next to her.

Kendra's eyebrow arched.

Rick gave her a crooked grin. "Seriously, we just left the office at the same time."

"If you say so." Kendra chuckled. "What if we stay for a couple of drinks and then go somewhere to talk? I mean, if you don't have to drive her home, or anything."

Kendra was baiting him. She didn't believe he was here on his own and was trying to catch him in a lie. Fine, he'd go, just to prove her wrong.

"Okay. Two drinks, then we'll leave."

"You can leave first. I'll follow a little later. Nobody has to know."

"Does it matter?"

She smirked. "Not to me. But you're the one with a date, not to mention being the big man in charge. Maybe it matters to you?" Her eyes held a challenge.

His blood simmered. He never responded well to having his integrity questioned. "Let's go now." Rick settled his tab and tossed a handful of bills down for the tip. He turned and took Kendra's arm, escorting her through the crowd to the front door. He pushed aside a mental image of pressing her up against the door and kissing her hard enough to make her cling to him and gasp for breath. His muzzled conscience wailed behind his libido, warning him not to leave the bar with her.

Chapter Fourteen

They walked back to the FBI building in silence. Rick opened his passenger door for her, and Kendra slid into the seat. He went around to his side, pulling in a deep breath on the way. "So, where do you want to go?" he asked as he folded his large frame into the car. "I'm not familiar with any nice restaurants in the area yet."

"Let's go downtown." As he drove, Kendra told him where to turn, making their way across the city. LoDo, Denver's lower downtown district, was known for its trendy shopping and dining scene. Near Union Station, Larimer Square, with lights strung across the street, encompassed an historic block with elegant Victorian buildings, trendy boutiques, and gourmet restaurants. She directed him to the Capital Grille.

They dropped the Explorer off with valet parking and stepped inside an elegant foyer. A hostess seated them in a quiet corner of the steak house by a fireplace, at a table with a white tablecloth set with fine china.

Rick pulled out a chair for Kendra. "Looks like a nice place. Do you eat here a lot?"

"No—never actually. I always wanted to try it, but I chose it tonight because I heard it was a quiet place with good food, and figured we could talk more easily." Kendra spread her napkin across her lap. "I'm not really dressed for this restaurant though." She slid her hand up and surreptitiously pulled the elastic out of her hair, allowing the waves to cascade over her shoulders.

"You look great." It was ironic. Here was this naturally breath-stealing woman concerned she didn't dress well enough to impress the diners in the ritzy restaurant. Did she really not know she could show up in a bathrobe and outshine them all? His imagination immediately supplied him with an image of her wearing only a robe. He bit down on his lip.

Their waiter appeared, and Kendra ordered a Cabernet. Rick asked for an IPA and when the drinks came, he touched his glass to hers. "*Salud*."

"Cheers." She raised her crystal goblet to him.

"So..."

She smiled at him and tilted her head to the side. "So... what are we doing?"

Rick thought about pretending he didn't understand what she meant, but she'd seen through him already. "I don't know, exactly. I mean... there's obviously an attraction, but — "

"But what? Is there someone special in your life? Do you have something going with Lucinda?" The vulnerability in her expression slapped him hard.

He took two slugs of his beer before he was ready to answer. "No." He had to be strong. It was wrong to lead her down a path he couldn't stay on. "Frankly, I don't have room for anyone in my life right now." He cleared his throat. "It's why I haven't asked you out before. I didn't want to give you the idea that I was looking for a relationship."

One dark brow rose high on her forehead under the still present, though faded bruise. "Is that so?"

Wait—the tone in her voice warned him this wasn't going the way he thought it would. Rick was uncertain. "Well, yeah."

"How nice of you to decide for me what I want." Kendra flipped a length of hair behind her shoulder. "Maybe I'm only looking for a short-term physical thing. After all, you don't know. You never asked me."

Rick drew his brows together. *Wait. What?* He stared at her. "I didn't want to... I mean we work together. It could be awkward."

The look she gave him made Rick feel like a kinder-gartener who got caught trying to peek under a girl's hemline on the monkey bars. Her second brow rose to match the first. "I guess we'll never know."

The waiter arrived to take their dinner order then, and Kendra ordered a filet—medium rare. Rick hadn't even glanced at the menu, so he quickly ordered a New York strip simply to get rid of the man.

"It's just that I don't want to be in a relationship right now."

She laughed. "Good to know."

Genuinely confused, Rick sat back in his chair and stared at her.

She leaned forward, her forearms resting on the edge of the table. "Listen. I just wanted to clear the air. We are obvi-ously attracted to each other, but if you don't want to pursue anything, I get it. Now we can work together without the tension, right?"

Why did her words feel like a gut punch? "Right. Good." Rick sucked down the rest of his beer and nodded to the waiter to bring another. He allowed his mind the tiniest glimpse of a memory of Alyssa. The pain still so sharp, more than a glance at it was too much, especially in public. Rick clenched his jaw to fight off the crushing weight of his grief and the guilt that raged with it. His fresh lager arrived, and he downed half the glass.

"Whoa. We still have to drive back to the office." Kendra canted her head, her warm, concerned gaze soothed like cognac.

Rick's conscience mule-kicked him in the chest. He'd taken a long, booze-laden detour down a dark rabbit hole after Alyssa. After climbing back out, he made himself a promise never to anesthetize himself from pain with that particular drug again. "You're right. Sorry." He set the key-fob on the table. "I'm done, but to be safe, here's the key."

Kendra smiled then, and instead of reaching for the keys, she took his hand. "You're a good guy, you know that? I don't know what's going on with you, but if you ever want to talk, I'm here."

"Thanks." Rick pulled his fingers back. This woman was dangerous to the integrity of his carefully constructed wall. He felt stripped bare in front of her and it scared him. If only his attraction to her were purely physical, this would be simple.

"So, how's your head?" He aimed for safer ground. "Any lasting symptoms? The bruise is looking better." He schooled a bland expression to settle on his face.

Kendra assessed him with a knowing glint in her eyes and took a minute to answer. "Mostly, I feel fine, but sometimes I have nightmares about the incident." Their meals arrived, the rich scent of grilled meat causing his mouth to water. After the first few bites accompanied by groans of appreciation for well-cooked steak, Kendra continued. "It scares me to think of how vulnerable I was, lying there, unconscious in the presence of a serial killer." She closed her eyes briefly. "One who was cutting a bone out of a dead woman, twenty feet away from me. It makes me sick that I couldn't stop him."

A sense of protectiveness swelled inside his chest. Rick

resisted his desire to reach for her and pull her into his arms, promising to keep her safe. "Maybe you shouldn't be involved with this case. You're too close and I'm sure the evidence brings up a lot of bad feelings."

"No way. I want to help catch this bastard." Her knuckles whitened as she gripped her steak knife and attacked her filet with a vengeance.

"I understand that. But if it gets to be too much, will you back off?"

"I don't think working on the case is aggravating me. Honestly, the nightmares only involve that sense of being completely at his mercy. If you can use that term in regard to a murderer."

"You still don't remember seeing his face?"

She shook her head.

"No faces appear in your nightmares?" If they had any clues at all they could move forward. "We need something to go on besides another murder."

Rick's phone buzzed in his pocket. He wasn't inclined to answer it when he was eating dinner. It was a small thing, but he tried to maintain that boundary. When it vibrated again, he knew he had to take the call. He pulled the device out and checked the screen. "Excuse me."

Kendra obviously read his phone upside down and leaned forward, watching Rick's face as he fielded the call. He clicked off and met her gaze directly. "There's been another murder."

She wiped her mouth and laid the napkin across her plate. "Let's go."

"No. I'll take you back to your car and then I'll go."

"I want to go with you."

The muscles in his neck and back went rigid. "That's not a good idea."

"Why not? I'm working the case too. I'm going with you."

Rick crushed his molars together and nodded once. He pulled several bills out of his wallet and tossed them on the table before stepping over to their waiter to explain. His whole system rebelled at the thought of taking Kendra with him to the crime scene, but he followed her to the car.

Chapter Fifteen

✦✦✦

Kendra drove, even though Rick was technically fine. It was always better to play it safe. She liked that he was on the same page as she was in that regard. Rick plotted the GPS coordinates that dispatch sent him. By the time they pulled into the location of the crime, huge flood lights were in place illuminating the scene.

"My God, Rick. This is the dog park where we were last weekend." Kendra swallowed against the bile rising in her throat. These murders were too close to home.

Rick opened his door. "Yeah, you're right, and the bastard is escalating."

"Assuming it's the same guy." Kendra got out and walked with him to the junior 'scribe' officer, their steps crunching on the gravel pathway. They signed into the crime scene before ducking under the yellow tape. "This makes three murders in Colorado."

"And all only weeks apart. It was a year between the first and second victims. We didn't make the serial murder connection until the third woman who was killed also had a missing rib."

"Then there was Kansas."

"Right, and months passed between those three incidents. Now three more murders, all bunched together." Rick stopped five feet from the body. Standing side by side, they stared at the victim under the bright halogen light. The blood on her clothing and in her hair appeared black in the glare. Rick perched his hands on his hips and swung his gaze to her. "Three—in one town. But why? Does he have a Colorado connection?" He paced. "Does he live here? Have family here?"

Kendra covered her mouth and nose with her hand in a vain attempt to block the vague, sickly sweet odor of death from penetrating her senses. She slid her phone from her pocket, pressed several buttons on the screen and held the device to her ear. "Cameron, it's Dean. Are you still at the bar?"

"No, I came straight to the office after getting the call."

"Good. As soon as we get confirmation on the identity of this current victim, you'll need to start looking for a connection between the three women." On the surface, there wasn't one. The women were not related, and their friends and family had never heard of the others. But there *had* to be something. Something they were missing. "We have to figure out not only why he's remaining in this location, but why he's ramped up his pace—before he kills anyone else."

"I'm on it."

"Thanks." She clicked off and Rick nodded, chewing his lip. "This is the third murder victim discovered on your side of town, Kendra, and I don't like it." He turned to face her. "When you were attacked, the guy stole your weapon, right?"

"Yes." The hair on her neck prickled.

"Did he take anything else? The investigators found nothing besides your water bottle at the scene."

Kendra closed her eyes and tried to picture that day. Her

memory was still a bit hazy, but she strained to focus. Had she been carrying anything? Ice water flooded her veins and her jaw dropped open.

"Oh, shit." She clutched Rick's arm to steady herself. "I had a pack. I don't usually carry one, but that day, I brought my lunch and Bax's collapsible travel bowl."

"Was there anything else in the pack?" Rick's eyes, black in the night, searched hers.

Kendra's body drooped and Rick gripped both of her shoulders to keep her on her feet. Kendra stared into his face. "He's got a set of my keys."

"Fuck! All this time?" Rick's jaw muscles bulged and his grip tightened on her arms. "That maniac has your keys? Does that mean your house key too?"

"Yes, I guess." Her head swam, and she felt foolish for not remembering before now. "But he doesn't know where I live, so the keys won't do him any good."

Rick stared at her and his brows scrunched. "Kendra, you've been all over the news. It only takes a simple Google search and a little persistence to find you. You're an FBI agent, you should know that."

"True, but the only address I have posted anywhere is a post office box. He can't find me unless he hacks the post office records."

Rick spun around and stalked off. He walked about ten feet before he turned back. "I don't like it. I don't want you going home."

"Rick. None of this is about me. I just happened along— the wrong place at the wrong time. This guy has an agenda. If I were a part of it, I'd already be dead. He would have killed me that day in the woods. Right now, we should focus on the murder at hand."

Rick called a uniformed cop over. "I need someone to drive Agent Dean to the FBI Headquarters." He turned to her. "You go with this officer. I'll have Cameron meet you at the front door."

Kendra narrowed her eyes. Her head blazed with a hot anger that melted downward over her shoulders and settled in the pit of her belly. "You don't have the authority to remove me from this case, Sanchez. I'm not going anywhere."

"Damn it, Kendra. I'm trying to keep you safe. We don't know where this bastard is, or who he's going to go after next." Agitated, Rick scanned the darkness that surrounded them.

Her fingers curled into fists. "I can take care of myself. I'm a god-damned federal agent, not your great aunt Martha."

Rick's eyes held an angry flame in the depths of their darkness. His expression was harsh and intense, his voice, when he spoke was low and lethal. "I *do* have the authority." He nodded at the officer who took Kendra by the arm.

The heat in her stomach ignited, and the blaze caught in her throat. She yanked her arm away from the uniformed cop, but she went with him, figuring Rick would sooner have her arrested than allow her to stay with him at the crime scene. She hesitated, looking over her shoulder. "After this, you're done making decisions for me, Agent Sanchez." Kendra shuddered with the adrenaline of her fury. *Who the hell does he think he is?*

———

ABBOT PEERED THROUGH HIS NIGHT VISION SCOPE. THERE she was. Just like he figured—even hoped, if he was honest. That was the problem. He couldn't stop thinking about her, and Abbot didn't know why God kept throwing her in his path. It must be a divine message. The woman hadn't recognized him at the dog park the other day, but he remembered her... and her dog.

That was more than a coincidence. He'd been scoping out easily accessible wilderness spots when she drove right up and parked next to his van. It had to be God, serving her up to him like a sacrificial lamb. He would have taken her too, if that other man hadn't shown up. Abbot could have figured out what his mission was regarding her by now, if that guy wasn't always sniffing around. Of course, that's what women like her did to men. Bewitched them. Made men want to touch them. Then lured them into committing awful sins. Abbot shuddered.

His daddy's sermons echoed through his skull. *"Women tempt men, trick them, and draw them straight into hell."* He peered through the lenses and whispered, *"For the lips of an immoral woman are as sweet as honey, and her mouth is smoother than oil. But in the end she is as bitter as poison, as dangerous as a double-edged sword. Her feet go down to death, her steps lead straight to the grave. For she cares nothing about the path to life. She staggers down a crooked trail and doesn't realize it."*

The fall of man wasn't Adam's fault. He gets the blame, but it was, in fact, Eve. The man's own wife tricked him into the grave. Just like Abbot's own mother did to his daddy. It wasn't Daddy's fault—the things he did. *God knows that and has bestowed upon me this quest for vengeance. Daddy said so.*

Perhaps the cop was wise to this daughter of Eve. It looked as though he was sending her away. Interesting. He took a second to send a positive thought toward the policeman who escorted her to his squad car. Hopefully, he would escape her treacherous wiles.

With his next breath, Abbot realized he was being given a divinely afforded opportunity to find out where this Jezebel lived. On his way to the van, he patted the ring of keys that he'd been carrying in his front pocket—the set he found in her backpack. Her gun he kept hidden in the glove compartment, just in case. Once he followed her home, he would wait until she slept before he visited upon her the wrath she deserved.

Twitchy with anticipation, he sped down the hill to the base of the valley where the dog park was located. He had to catch up with the squad car before they got on the highway. He careened down the dirt road to where it met pavement and stepped on the accelerator. He searched the streets ahead, but didn't see anyone. The cop car was gone. They could have driven in a number of directions. Abbot's vision blurred with the edge of his frustration.

She wouldn't get away that easily. He'd look her up on a computer. *She might think she's more clever than me, but she's wrong.* In his mind's eye, Abbot conjured an image of himself waiting for her in her bedroom when she got home. *No. Not her bedroom. Her powers could overtake me there. Daddy warned me about that. I have to stop her before she has a chance to cast her spell.*

Abbot drove north until he found the library. He entered and asked the librarian for help. She led him to the computer section and signed him on. It pleased him that not all women were treacherous. The old lady wore no perfume or makeup. She had short gray hair and glasses. Her unpainted fingernails were cut short. She barely looked at him while she did as she was told.

"Thank you."

"Of course. The library closes in forty-five minutes." She went back to her task of checking in books.

Abbot sat in front of the screen and searched for articles about the adulteress he had sacrificed who was stumbled upon by a federal agent. He found four articles, but only two of them had photos. There were no pictures of the agent, but he wasn't discouraged, because in the fourth article the reporter quoted her. *Special Agent Kendra Dean.*

A smile turned up the corners of his mouth. *Got her.* Next, he ran a search using her name. He looked for her workplace, her address, her phone. He hit dead-end after dead-end. Finally, he found his way to a website that verified identities. After creating a false email account, he had the information sent there. All he had to do was click a button that asked if he agreed to only use the information he found in an ethical and legal manner. Abbot almost laughed out loud. He would have if he wasn't in a library where making noise was against the rules.

Abbot's plans were above ethics and legality. He received them by divine order.

"I'm sorry, sir, but the library is now closing." The librarian was back. Abbot quickly closed the tab. He'd have to return tomorrow to open his fake email and retrieve the information he needed. For now he was content to roll the name *Kendra Dean* around on his tongue. Tomorrow was fine. He had all the time in the world.

Besides, he was anxious to get back to his motel. It was time to cleanse. He rented a room by the week that included a mini-fridge, hot-plate, and a microwave. It had everything he required. Even the other occupants were perfect neighbors. Most of them were strung out and wouldn't remember seeing an avenging angel living among them.

He pulled his van into the cracked and pitted parking lot and parked around the backside of the motel, away from the lights of the street. Inside his room, he bolted and chained his door closed and checked that there was no gap in the drapes. He filled a pot with water and set it on the hot plate, turning the burner to high.

While the water heated, Abbot stripped naked. He pulled a sheet from the bed and spread it on the floor. Kneeling in the center, he gripped his cat-o'-nine-tails, the one Daddy used on him before he died, and flung it hard over his shoulder and across his back. The leather knots broke open scabs from previous cleansings and bit into fresh skin. Tears burned in his eyes, but he must not cry out. He breathed in, and gritting his teeth, he swung again.

Muttering under his breath, Abbot choked out the words. *"The righteous will rejoice when he sees the vengeance; He will wash his feet in the blood of the wicked. And men will say, 'Surely there is a reward for the righteous; Surely there is a God who judges on earth.'"*

Sweat dripped down his face and mingled with tears, yet he struck again. *"Behold, I was brought forth in iniquity, and in sin my mother conceived me... Purify me with hyssop, and I shall be clean. Wash me, and I shall be whiter than snow... Let the bones which You have broken rejoice."*

Twelve lashes later, Abbot fell forward onto his hands and braced himself until he caught his breath. He turned off the burner under the boiling water and mixed in half a bottle of rubbing alcohol. Carrying the pot with him, he stepped into the bathtub. This was the worst part, but it would be over soon and Abbot would be prepared to sacrifice the next whore.

Abbot tucked his chin to his chest and raised the pot above his head. Tilting it, he poured the scorching liquid down his back, searing the wounds and purifying himself. With all his might, he tried not to cry out, but his body rebelled and he screamed as the hot alcohol mixture burned his tender skin. Sometimes, he passed out at this point in his ritual, but tonight he was strong. He was ready.

Chapter Sixteen

✣✣✣

Agent Cameron pulled into the parking garage as the burgeoning coral-edge of dawn trembled on the horizon. He'd promised Sanchez he'd get an early start organizing all the evidence they'd been compiling onto the murder board. The lab came back with DNA results from the first two Colorado victims. It proved that the same man killed both women, but the coding didn't match any DNA previously recorded in the FBI CODIS system. All that told them was the murderer hadn't been arrested before. Without a match, they had no identity. The only way the DNA results could help them now, was in court—*after* they caught the bastard.

Burke stepped out of the elevators and noticed a light shining from the far end of the cubicles. He checked his watch. Just after five thirty in the morning. His fingers grazed the grip of his pistol as he crept down the hallway toward the lit room. Something heavy hit the floor in the conference room, startling Burke with both the bang and its vibration. He dashed to the wall and peered in through the door.

The tension drained from his muscles. "Dean. What the

hell are you doing here so early? I thought you were an intruder."

Kendra spun around to face him. "An intruder? Inside the FBI building? Not likely."

Heat spiraled up Burke's neck. He'd overreacted. Thank God he hadn't come in with his gun drawn. He'd have never heard the end of it. "Why are you here?" He noted that she was wearing the same clothes as yesterday. "Did you stay here all night?"

Her jaw set and she tilted her chin. "Agent Sanchez is too possessive over this case. Can you believe he made that uniform bring me back here last night? I want to see all the new evidence we have before he has a chance to push me out of the mix again today."

"Does he think you're too close to the case, or what?" Burke had a bit of professional hero worship aimed at Agent Sanchez and wanted to defend him if necessary. The whole team sensed the undercurrent between Dean and Sanchez, but they didn't yet know if it was interest or dislike.

Kendra dropped a stuffed six-inch binder on the table with a loud clap. "He thinks he's protecting me. Which really pisses me off. Sanchez is no more of an agent than I am. I have the same training."

"But wasn't he a Marine before that?"

"So what, Cameron? I was in the Army."

"Yeah, but..." Burke glanced around for something to use to change the direction of this conversation. Kendra tended to get heated when she felt like she had to defend her competence as an agent. "Is that the murder book?"

"Whatever, Cameron. You know I can take care of myself. I'm pissed that he dismissed me from the crime scene like a civilian." She slapped open the cover of the notebook and took a deep breath. "Yes, this is the book. Let's get started pinning the new stuff to the wall."

Burke nodded, but kept his mouth shut. More words would not help. He and Kendra worked side by side posting the evidence for the next hour, trying to string together any connections.

———

AT SEVEN, THE ELEVATOR DOORS DINGED. KENDRA CLOSED her eyes and breathed in the invigorating scent of dark-roasted coffee in one long inhale. She kept her lids closed and sniffed the aroma again.

Rick entered the conference room carrying a drink tray filled with paper coffee cups. He raised a box of pastries over his head. "Sustenance has arrived." His gaze settled on Kendra. His eyes narrowed slightly and a muscle bulged on in his jaw. "I didn't know you were coming in this early, Dean. Good thing I brought extra coffee."

How can a man who was up most of the night with a murder investigation show up first thing in the morning looking so damn fine? Rick's face was clean shaven, his neck swarthy against his starched white collar and snug electric blue tie. Kendra smoothed her hair and bit down on the inside of her lips, hoping to get a flush of color to them. "Yeah, thanks. It smells fabulous." She reached for a cup. "I've been here since last night."

His gaze lingered long enough to birth tension in the room before he turned to Burke. "Connect any more dots, Cameron?"

Burke glanced at Kendra furtively before he answered. "Uh, Agent Dean came up with a few things."

She understood that Burke was attempting to include her, maybe even elevate her position in Agent Sanchez's fathomless eyes, but the fact that he felt he needed to was, in itself, infuriating. Her work and her record could speak for itself.

When Rick's gaze panned to her, his brows raised in question, she swallowed her irritation and tried for a professional tone.

"Cameron and I discussed how all the victims are women in their twenties. All were found in the wilderness, some distance away from where they were abducted. Some were likely killed at the scene, some were dead before they got there." Kendra sipped her coffee and approached the wall. "The murderer smashed all the victims' skulls with a rock and cut each of their bottom left ribs from their bodies at the scene—postmortem. None of the women show any signs of rape. All were strangled to death. The two who were married had their wedding rings stuffed into their throats."

"None of that is new information." Rick leaned forward and braced his arms on the conference table. Kendra couldn't help appreciating his forearm muscles flexing under his rolled-up cuffs, but quickly cleared her throat to continue.

"So, let's compress it. Young, arguably attractive women, strangled to death, skulls crushed with a rock, stolen ribs— one particular rib—found in the wilderness. Married women facing even further insult."

Rick stood and crossed his arms. He stared at the evidence on the wall. "What are you getting at, Dean?"

Kendra let out a sigh. "I don't know... there is something, almost... well, biblical about all of it."

"Biblical?" Rick stared at her.

Burke stepped forward. "It's just a hunch, sir, but a woman stoned to death, missing a rib, and left in the wilderness. Do you think it means anything?"

Rick cocked his jaw sideways and rubbed it with his hand. His black eyes surveyed the evidence again. "Could be. It's something anyway." He pulled a paper cup out of the tray and opened the lid to add cream. "Good work. Keep at it. I have a meeting with the SAC in fifteen. The evidence from last night's murder should be back from the lab in a couple of hours. Let me know if you come up with anything else." He snapped the plastic cover back onto his coffee cup. "Burke, you and Stott get over to the victim's home and interview the family."

"It's Stott's day off. Want me to take Dean?"

Rick turned to go, but let his gaze pause on Kendra. He contemplated her for a minute, then nodded once and left.

"What the hell was that about?" Burke opened the box of pastries and pulled out a donut with sprinkles.

Kendra snatched the confection from Burke's hand and bit into it. "Who knows?" she said, grinning around the dough.

"Hey!" Burke laughed and picked out another. "That was the only one with sprinkles."

"Aww." Kendra teased, glad she diverted the topic she was wondering about herself, but for which she had no answers. The power of Rick's gaze lingered in the form of a warm glow in her belly. No matter how pissed off at him she was, she couldn't help imagining all the ways he could use that intensity.

Chapter Seventeen

Kendra followed the directions from Google Maps on the screen in her dashboard and pulled up in front of a small brick house in Aurora. Worn to dust, what might have once been a lawn in front of the home was gone. Still, unlike many of the other houses in the neighborhood, this one seemed cared for. Trash cans stood side by side, snugged up to the outer wall of the house at the edge of a cement drive where an ancient, faded gold, Dodge Dart parked. There was no garage or carport attached to cover the car.

"Ready?" she asked Burke as she scanned the street up and down. This was the type of area that required agents to watch each other's backs.

"Let's do it." Burke opened his door and stepped out onto the sidewalk. He waited for Kendra to come around the car, and they walked together to the front door. Decorative iron bars, painted cream to match the trim, covered the windows and the heavy screen door was locked with a deadbolt.

Kendra pressed the doorbell. A moment later, a rattling sounded on the other side of the door as it was unchained and pulled open. A short, round woman wearing thick glasses and a curly black, plastic-looking wig stared at them.

"Yes?"

"Mrs. Johnson?" Kendra held up her badge and ID.

The woman peered through her lenses. "You cops?"

"Sort of, ma'am. We're actually with the FBI. I'm Agent Dean and this is Agent Cameron." Kendra held up her badge and ID. "Do you mind if we come in and talk with you about your daughter?"

Mrs. Johnson let out a great sigh and reached for the lock on the screen door. "I suppose. Come on in." She stood back and held the door while Kendra and Burke entered a small, but neatly kept living room. The deadbolt clicked back in its slot and the chain clinked into its slide behind them.

"Have a seat. Would you like some coffee?"

Kendra's heart squeezed. "No, thank you." This poor woman just found out that someone murdered her daughter and yet she offered hospitality. "First, we'd like to express how sorry we are about your daughter's death." Kendra sat on the green and gold velveteen couch next to Mrs. Johnson and Burke took an end chair.

The woman dabbed her swollen eyes, with a handkerchief she slid underneath her glasses. "I just can't believe it. Tansey was going to make it out of here. Such a bright girl. She wanted to be a nurse, did you know?"

"I didn't know that. She must have been a truly caring person." Kendra squeezed Mrs. Johnson's hand. "Do you know if Tansey had classes, at..." She flipped open her notepad to check her information, "Arapahoe Community College, yesterday?"

Mrs. Johnson nodded but held her hankie in front of her mouth. Her shoulders jerked with silent sobs. Kendra rubbed the back of her shoulder. "I'm sorry, Mrs. Johnson. I understand this is difficult, but do you know if she had plans to meet anyone after her last class? Or did she call to tell you she'd be home later than usual?"

"No. She was going to come straight home because we were supposed to go to my sister's for dinner. Only she never called…" A wracking sob shook the woman's body. "Never came home."

The police found Tansey Johnson's car in the school's parking lot, with her purse on the driver's seat, and the car door left unlocked. Tansey's keys were on the floor mat, and her credit card was inside her purse along with twenty-eight dollars in cash. It certainly didn't look like she'd been robbed. Considering the meticulously locked door on the house, Kendra found it hard to imagine that the young woman would leave her purse in an unlocked car, either.

"Can you give us the names and numbers of Tansey's close friends? We'd like to see if she called any of them, or if anyone saw her leave the school."

"She didn't have many friends, but I'll give you what I have." Mrs. Johnson trundled into the kitchen and returned with an old-fashioned, metal address file. She slid the pointer to the B's and snapped the cover open. Five names were meticulously penciled on the manila card. "Mikayla Brown was her closest friend, but she wouldn't have seen her at school. Mikayla works at the Walgreens during the day."

Kendra copied the number down in her small notebook. "Thank you. We'll give her a visit, anyway. They may have spoken on the phone." Tansey's phone was currently in evidence at the crime lab. It wouldn't be long before they knew exactly who Tansey spoke with, and when.

Burke cleared his throat. "Did your daughter mention any new friends or acquaintances she'd made recently?"

Mrs. Johnson slowly shook her head. "Tansey was so focused—determined to do well in school."

Burke stood and crossed the room to a photo of a beautiful young woman in a dark blue cap and gown. "Is this Tansey?" He picked up the frame. Mrs. Johnson nodded. "Do you mind if I take a picture of this photo on my phone?"

"Not if you think it will help."

"Thank you." He clicked a button on his screen.

Kendra reached forward and placed her hand over the woman's fingers that twisted a handkerchief in her lap and gave them a squeeze. "We're doing everything we can to find the person who did this." She handed Mrs. Johnson a business card. "Please call me at this number if you think of anything, anything at all, that might help."

The agents rose together and made their way to the door. "Thank you for talking with us."

Mrs. Johnson went through the routine of unbolting the doors. "You just find Tansey's murderer."

Burke ducked his head on the way out the door. "Yes, ma'am. We'll do our best."

THEY BOTH SAT IN THE CAR, STARING FORWARD THROUGH the windshield, deep in their own thoughts. Finally, Kendra snapped her seatbelt closed. "That poor woman."

Burke swiped his hand across his jaw. "Yeah, I'm beginning to see why interviewing the family of victims is the worst part of the job. It's hard to watch their pain."

"It motivates me to find the killer." Kendra pushed the start button on the SUV. "Other than being a beautiful young woman, I can't think of any possible connections between Tansey and the other victims. Tansey is the second African American victim. She was at school, in broad daylight, as far as we know, and nothing was stolen from her."

"So, can we assume her murder was not racially motivated? It doesn't seem like the victims knew their attacker. I think our killer is hunting young, attractive women. Maybe it's just that simple."

Kendra bit her lip. "We shouldn't assume anything. But the rib thing... there's got to be more to his motive, and if we can figure that out, we might have a chance of catching him before he strikes again." Kendra had that niggling feeling at the base of her skull she got when she was on to something, but couldn't quite get her mind around the details yet. It usually thrilled her. This was why she became an agent, the excitement of finding the puzzle pieces and figuring out how they fit together. But now, with innocent lives on the line, the tension was overwhelming.

Chapter Eighteen

Rick heard Kendra and Burke talking when they came through the doors. He'd been waiting for their return, anxious to know what they'd learned. "Cameron, Dean, meet me in the conference room in ten minutes." He called out. Burke waved a hand in acknowledgement.

All morning Rick had tried to evict thoughts of Kendra from his mind. He'd catch himself picturing her long, silky brown hair sliding over her shoulder or her smart-assed grin and her eyes sparkling with topaz mischief. Once, another agent asked why he was smiling to himself. *I need to get a grip.*

The truth was, he needed to go out on a meaningless date with someone he didn't really care about. He needed to get his mind off of Kendra. She stirred something deep and raw in his demolished heart. He wouldn't survive if he let anyone in there again. That wounded place was set aside as a shrine to Alyssa. It was hers. His heart would have been hers forever, if she had lived. Rick ran a hand over his face and shook his head hard. *Enough.*

He gathered up the file he'd been studying and went to

meet his team down the hall. On his way he passed by Lucinda's desk. He hesitated and glanced at her. Long red nails clicked rapidly on her keyboard. Her fingers paused.

"Do you need something?" Lucinda's sultry smile, painted a matching red, suggested she'd be happy to give him whatever he wanted.

"No—sorry. Just lost in thought."

"I can't help but wonder what type of thoughts put that hungry look in your eye."

Hungry? Yeah, that was the fault of a certain agent he couldn't get out of his brain. "Must be that I forgot to have lunch."

"Hmm. Well, since you're here, I wanted to see if you were busy later, after work?"

Here was his chance, Lucinda was sumptuous and willing. Only he shouldn't indulge in a casual distraction with someone at work. "Not sure. I think it's going to be a late work night."

"Well, if you do get off at a reasonable hour, maybe we could grab a drink?"

"I'll let you know."

KENDRA'S SKIN TINGLED WHEN RICK ENTER THE ROOM. SHE did her best not to look in his direction, but the subtle, sandalwood aftershave he wore refused to be ignored. Her stomach muscles tightened. When she did look up, she met his dark eyes and the electricity that shot out of them caused her to draw a sharp breath. She dropped her gaze immediately to the papers in her hand, hoping he didn't notice the reaction her body had to his.

Burke looked from Rick to Kendra and back. He cleared his

throat and spoke to the room. "Dean and I met with Tansey Johnson's mother this morning. We didn't learn anything new, though I got the name and phone number of her best friend. I'll contact her this afternoon. Any interesting results from the lab?"

Kendra felt Rick's charged stare. He'd look away for seconds at a time, but then his searing gaze would return. *What the actual hell?* She disciplined her own focus on the agents who spoke, though her skin burned under Rick's scrutiny.

Agent Stott presented the lab results. Same DNA found at the other crime scenes, no unusual phone calls or texts on the victim's phone. "The ME report shows bruises and contusions consistent with a struggle on the vic's knees and upper arms, along with bruising on the neck from manual strangulation." He glanced up at the group. "We have enough evidence to link the same killer to all of these crimes. If we find him, he's going down."

Rick shot a quick look toward Stott. "Not if—*when*."

Stott shrugged. "Yeah—when."

The agents stood at various points around the room, all staring at the wall of evidence. Kendra's mind strained to find a hidden clue, something that would give them a direction. She was still contemplating the photos of the victims when she realized that it was five-thirty, and everyone else had left. Everyone except Rick.

His deep voice skittered up her spine and out through her nervous system. "You've been staring at the board for almost an hour. Any new ideas? Thoughts?" He stood next to her, folded his arms, and leaned back against the conference table. They both stared at the wall.

"No, and it's so damn frustrating."

"I've been wondering why this guy takes his victims out to Chatfield every time. Two things have changed since he started his spree. The increased frequency, and that he's returning to the same location."

Kendra nodded and glanced at him sideways. "The women are from all over the metro area. No racial connections, no socio-economic connections. It doesn't seem to make sense, but he's so methodical in his attack method that it makes me feel like we're missing something."

"I agree, random doesn't fit with his structured routine. What aren't we seeing?"

"He drugs a woman, abducts her, and strangles her. Then he drives out to the wilderness around the reservoir to dump the body. He smashes her skull with a rock and cuts out a rib before folding her hands together on her chest."

Kendra turned to face Rick. "Those things are consistent every time. Same with his earlier murders too, right?"

"Yep." Rick's dark eyes settled on her. "What are you thinking?"

"I keep getting stuck on the biblical feel to this. It's like the women have been sent out to the wilderness. Maybe the crushed skull symbolizes being stoned to death? Maybe these women did something that our killer thinks is worthy of being put to death?" Kendra let out a pent-up breath. "It's like a perverted version of ancient old-testament justice. We should get a bible. Maybe we can figure out what sins merited being cast out and stoned."

"What about the rib, though?"

Kendra groaned. "I don't know. I'm grasping at straws as it is." She bent to gather her papers and notebook. "It's late." She stepped toward the door.

RICK REACHED HIS HAND OUT TO STOP HER. "HOLD ON."

The gold flecks in her eyes caught the light. "Yeah?" Her long, silky hair swung over her shoulder as she turned.

His heart echoed like a timpani drum against his sternum. *What the hell, Sanchez...* He pressed on though he felt like he had lost his mind. "I was wondering."

Her brow snapped up.

"Can we get a drink?"

Her brows dipped together over narrowed eyes.

"I want to explain what happened the other night." Rick shoved his hands in his pockets. "I don't know, maybe I want to try to understand it myself. All I know is, I can't stop thinking about you. I want to spend time with you... and I'm afraid."

"Afraid of what?"

"Pain."

Kendra understood that fear. She wasn't immune. It stung like hell when you let someone in and they took advantage of your trust—your vulnerability. She also couldn't deny that Rick occupied far more than his fair share of her thoughts. He was a man she wanted in her life, yet he gave off flashing warnings that he was an unstable choice.

She glanced at her watch. "It's already late, but if we keep it to just one drink..."

"Deal." He opened the conference room door for her and followed her out.

Chapter Nineteen

Rick pulled out a tall chair at the high-top table in the pub.

"Thank you." Kendra hung her purse on the back and slid onto the seat. She glanced around the place with her usual scan, noticing the people, any possible threats, and where the exits were all located.

"Thanks for coming." Rick made a similar purview of the room before he sat across from her. "I wasn't sure you would after the last time we went out."

"Dinner was great. It was the way you dismissed me from the crime scene later, that pissed me off." Kendra stared into the depth of his boundless eyes.

He held her gaze for a moment before he dropped his focus to his hands folded on the table. "I was probably a little harsh, but I can't help feeling that the location of these bodies has something to do with you."

"Why? I mean, if the killer was trying to threaten me, wouldn't he make it more obvious? Perhaps take his victims to the spot where he knocked me out?"

"Maybe."

The server stopped to take their order, and Rick waited for her to leave before he continued.

"The thing is, I've got a gut feeling about this, and I always trust my gut. I don't believe for one minute that it's simply a coincidence that the killer left those bodies in the same dog park you take Baxter to."

If she were honest, she would admit she agreed with him. The truth was the whole situation had her spooked, but she was a professional. "It doesn't matter. You can't treat me like a china doll. I deserve to be a part of this investigation. I can handle myself and I need you to believe that."

Rick stared at her, the bunched muscles in his jaw flexed. Finally, he looked away and cleared his throat. "I know." His voice was low and almost impossible to hear.

"What is it? Are you afraid to start a relationship with me because you've got a feeling I'm going to get hurt? Is that it?" Kendra reached forward and placed her hand on his.

He moved his thumb to caress her fingers and hold them there. "I want to tell you something, but it's hard for me to talk about. It's even harder for me to think about." His pain-filled gaze flashed up to her. "About three years ago, I was engaged."

Kendra's belly cinched, but she kept her face passive.

"Her name was Alyssa Martin." Rick's Adam's apple bobbed. "She was my life. And..." He paused so long Kendra wondered if he would finish. "It was my fault that she was killed."

Whatever Kendra thought he was going to say, that was not it. "Oh, Rick. I'm so sorry. You don't have to talk about it if you don't want to. I get it."

"I didn't think I'd ever want to be serious with anyone, ever again, so I haven't talked about it much. I don't really want to, but I think it's only fair for you to be able to under-stand me."

Kendra set her other hand on top of his and squeezed. "Okay, I'm here. Take your time." Her chest ached at the visible grief that washed through his eyes and over his face.

Rick dipped his head. "We'd been out at a movie when I got a call to go to a crime scene connected to a case that I'd been working on." He swallowed and stared at the table. "We were on the other side of Chicago from her apartment and the crime scene was only about a ten-minute drive." He glanced up at Kendra. The grief that pooled in his eyes stabbed her heart. "I knew better. It was lazy... but I drove to the location and told Alyssa to stay in the car." A sob escaped his throat and Kendra gripped his hands tight.

He flashed her a wobbly grin. "She never did what she was told. I admired her feistiness." He pulled in a deep breath. "Anyway, I went to find my partner. Actually, you know him— Jack Stone. You met him in Idaho."

Kendra nodded, remembering the missing agent she helped find, but she said nothing, allowing Rick the time and space he needed.

"While I spoke with him, my back was to my car. All of a sudden, Jack shoved me aside and dropped to a knee." Rick stared off into the distance as though he was reliving the scenario all over again. "He fired his gun. My ears rang. I thought he'd busted my eardrum, but I spun to see what he shot at." Rick closed his eyes and bumps scattered across Kendra's skin. She shivered.

Rick continued. "A man, who we later proved killed the woman at the scene, had rushed out from the bushes. He grabbed Alyssa and held a blade to her throat. When Jack saw him, he leveled his gun at the bastard. Then, without hesitating, the psycho..." he couldn't finish.

Kendra waited. The waitress brought their drinks and sensing the mood, set them on the table and left. Finally, Kendra spoke. "He killed her?"

"Sliced her throat, like it was nothing." He sat up and swallowed. "She fell, and Jack shot him. It was such a waste. So stupid." He wiped his eyes on his sleeve. "If only I would have taken her home first... Don't you see? If she wasn't there..."

"That is truly awful, Rick." She shook her head. "I'm so sorry. But there's no way you could have known. Murderers don't usually hang around while the cops are investigating."

"I went against protocol. My stupid decision cost Alyssa her life. I should have protected her." His eyes hardened and his jaw bulged. "I'm not about to let that happen again. So, when I get a bad feeling in my gut about victims found at a dog park you frequent, one that isn't very far from where you live, I listen to it." He stretched his hand across the table and grasped her forearm and moved to the chair next to hers. "Because I care."

Still unable to shake her self-defensiveness. "But Rick, this is different. I'm a federal agent. I'll bet you've never had one of your male counterparts removed from a crime scene, have you? Did you ever send Jack Stone away from an investigation?"

A wicked grin warmed Rick's face and his eyes sparked. "Well, no... but — "

"That's what I thought." She pulled her arm away.

"But I never did this to Jack either." Rick bent forward, and cupping the back of her head, he pressed his mouth firmly to hers, stealing her breath. He touched her forehead with his and looked her in the eyes. "*That's* why I sent you back to headquarters. Not because I don't think you can do your job, or that you can't defend yourself." His eyes searched hers.

Kendra's face heated and her heart expanded. "Oh."

Now, it was her turn in the confessional. Kendra pulled back and drew a long sip of her vodka tonic through the tiny cocktail straw. "It's just that all my life I've had to prove myself. I never measured up against my brother to my parents. And God knows I tried."

Rick scoffed. "Seriously? I think it's the other way around."

"Not in my parent's eyes. The thing is, I'm adopted. They brought me home as an infant after they couldn't get pregnant. My dad wanted a boy, but they got me instead. When I was little, he took me everywhere with him. We went fishing, watched ballgames, he let me sit on his workbench while he tinkered in his shop. Dad told everyone I was the son he never had."

Kendra sucked her drink dry, making a bubbly, slurping noise with her straw. "Then surprise. My mom got pregnant and she gave birth to Michael." She met Rick's eye. "That's all it took. A son—a boy of their own flesh and blood." She rushed on, not wanting Rick to think she felt sorry for herself. "Don't get me wrong. They're good people. I had a nice childhood—hell, far better than I could have had. I owe them everything."

She stabbed at the ice left in her glass. "All my life I've tried to make my parents proud of me. I got straight A's, excelled in track, but Michael was the star of the family. The thing is, I get it. I really do, but that never stopped me from trying to gain their approval.

"My dad had been a soldier, so after college I joined the Army. He was unimpressed, and all I accomplished was to put myself in a new situation where I had to prove my competence at work every day. The military is still a man's world." Kendra stopped talking, lost in her memories.

"Is the Army where you got involved with dogs?" Rick's question brought her back to the present.

"Yes. I loved the work, and my life was much more comfortable for me once I had my K9 partner with me twenty-four-seven. The guys who used to give me a hard time started keeping their distance. Not to mention that dogs are loyal and they always believe in you.

"Anyway, after the Army, I was accepted to the FBI Academy—but it was the same damn thing. My family doesn't believe I'm suited to be an agent. I'm so sick of having to prove that I'm good enough."

Rick shook his head. "You don't have to. Not to me, anyway. I've always thought of you as extremely competent. Kendra, the only person you have to prove yourself to, is you. I've always been impressed by your clarity and focus. You have a brilliant mind and can make calm decisions under extreme stress. You were instrumental in finding Jack when he was lost. *I'm* the one who started to panic." He reached for both of her hands. "Maybe your parents thought you weren't good enough, but you proved them wrong a long time ago. You have an impeccable reputation at the office among the other agents. You know that, right?"

Kendra's throat ached, and she shook her head. "Not really. I feel like I still have to prove myself, every day."

He slid his arm around her shoulders. "That's just not true. It's time to stop believing that lie. I wish I had a recording of the guys talking about you the week you were out. You have the respect of every agent there." He tipped her chin up and looked in her eyes. Kendra's cheeks burned, and she cast her gaze down into her lap. Did he think she was fishing for compliments?

He gave her a playful squeeze. "I have to say, your parents are crazy if they think your brother has anything at all over you. He's... I mean, he's a nice guy, but he's not..."

Kendra laughed at Rick belatedly trying to take back whatever derogatory statement he was going to make about Michael. She knew her brother was self-centered and cocky, but she loved him anyway, and nothing she could ever do would make her parents see her in the same glow as they saw him.

"Thanks. I appreciate all that you're saying."

They fell into an awkward silence. Rick kept his arm around her shoulders, his thumb tapped several times before he spoke. "So, now all that's out on the table, I think we understand each other a little better. Don't you?"

She nodded, resisting the urge to cuddle into the shelter of his chest and find the comfort she knew would be there.

"Then, do you think we could try seeing each other?"

"Officially?" she teased.

"Yeah."

"I'd like that." Kendra stopped resisting, and Rick drew her close. Her whole body relaxed into his. She wished they weren't in a public bar.

He kissed the top of her head and she pressed her cheek into his warmth. "Let's get out of here."

IT WAS SPRINGTIME, BUT THE NIGHT AIR WAS CRISP AND AS soon as they stepped outside, Kendra pulled her blazer snug and did up the buttons.

"You cold?" Rick slid his arm around her and drew her into his chest, rubbing his hands up and down her arms.

She tilted her chin up so she could see his face. "Thanks. It was nice today, but when the sun goes down, the temperature drops fast." She shivered.

"Want my jacket?" His voice vibrated through her body igniting a sultry glow.

"No, thanks. I like this though." She pressed into his hard chest.

"Want to walk a bit?"

Kendra kept her thoughts off what she *wanted* to do and said, "Sure. I'll probably warm up once we get moving."

Rick kept his arm around her and she felt the steady rhythm of his heart beating against her shoulder. They walked up the shop-lined block, stopping to peer in some of the windows, until they came to a small park at the end of the street. The green expanse was empty of people and they wandered until they found a bench to sit on.

"The stars sure are bright tonight." Rick stared at the sky.

"You should see them from my place. There's less light pollution out there and the stars seem bigger and closer."

Rick's gaze left the night sky and settled on her. Kendra's body softened under his study. When he touched her face, the jolt to her system felt like she'd been clipped to the hot end of a set of jumper cables, every nerve ending stood alert, anticipating more. He slid his hand up into her hair until his fingers found the back of her head and pulled her closer. His other hand cupped her throat and he caressed her jaw with his thumb. Rick's gaze smoothed over her lips and his mouth followed.

A hungry sound rose from her throat and his eyes darted to hers. He smiled that knowing grin she often recalled in her late-night thoughts and he kissed her again. This time, his mouth more insistent. He nibbled, nudging her lips with his and she parted them. He took full advantage of her acquiescence. His tongue tasted like bourbon. Kendra combed her fingers through his short, thick hair and pulled him closer, exploring. The pressure inside her body expanded like a helium balloon.

She edged back to catch her breath. "God..." she whispered.

His lips slid into the feline grin of a lion and his eyes sparked like those of a jungle cat stalking his prey. "I better get you back to your car." His words floated on the breeze without strength or conviction.

The next move was up to Kendra. With the slightest inclination, she would end up in Rick's bed. His apartment was only a few blocks away. She leaned in for another taste of him, and he kissed her with an intensity that communicated what he wanted her choice to be. Her body, in complete agreement with his, egged her on, a ravenous demand swirling through her abdomen. But this was too new and too soon. Reluctantly, her lungs drew in a deep breath of the cool night air.

"Yeah, I should get going. I have a long drive still." She kissed the side of his mouth.

Rick drew back slightly and studied her face. His gaze finally settling on hers. "Okay. But first—." His mouth covered hers once again, hard and demanding. The heat of his desire undisguised. For a long minute, Kendra lost herself in the sensuousness of his kiss.

Finally, she pulled away. "We have to stop," she said with a soft laugh. "I'll be lucky if I can walk after that kiss, let alone drive."

Rick's breath came fast and his jaw flexed. "Okay." He turned slightly and looked at her out the side of his eyes with a reluctant half smile. "If you say so."

Kendra reached up to touch the strong line of his cheekbone. "For now."

He pulled her hand to his mouth and, staring deep into her eyes, he kissed her palm.

Chapter Twenty

❧❧❧

The sun blazed across the bright blue Colorado sky as Abbot pulled into the King Soopers parking lot. He needed to stock up on food for the stake-out he planned for later. It had taken several days' worth of searching to locate the woman who'd been haunting his conscience. He should have followed her to her house from the dog park, but that man had shown up. Bitterness clogged his throat.

When Abbot finally found Special Agent Kendra Dean's name mentioned in a news article, he thought his hunt would get easier. But as far as he could tell, her home address was not recorded anywhere on the internet. Then hours of frustration later, Abbot uncovered a post office box listed under K.S. Dean in the small town of Sedalia, Colorado. That had to be her. After all, Sedalia was close to the mountains where he had first come upon her. Now all he had to do was sit and wait.

He pushed a grocery cart up the snack aisle, looking at the many colorful bags of chips. Frugality was the name of the game, since he had gone through most of his savings after he left Tennessee. He'd been living on a shoe-string, using the one credit card he had in his name. Abbot reached for a large bag of pretzels and a jar of Cheez Whiz to add to the white bread, bologna, and Coke already in his buggy. For dessert, he tossed in a box of Little Debbie's Moon Pies. At the last minute, he decided to include a piece of fruit to make his meal healthy.

He strolled through the produce section until he found the apple bins. *Fitting*, he thought. Abbot reached for the shiny, red fruit and accidentally bumped into a pretty blonde woman.

"Oh, excuse me." She smiled, blinking her large blue eyes.

A betraying grin played on his mouth in response to her. *I do not understand what I do. For what I want to do I do not do, but what I hate, I do.*

"I'm glad to see you're getting *something* healthy," she teased. "Look at what you have so far." The woman bent to peer into his cart and offered him a close-up view of her chest. She pointed at the jar of cheese. "This stuff isn't even real food, you know."

His body stirred, and in that moment, he despised his own flesh. This woman was like Bathsheba, exhibiting her nakedness to King David and tricking him into bed. Abbot's own mother had done the same thing to his daddy. In his hill-country church, Abbot's daddy preached about how it was a woman's nature to steal a man's power, to make him grovel for her. It all started in the beginning, with Eve.

He couldn't let that happen to him though. Abbot was called to be set apart, like Samson, only he wouldn't be fooled by any Delilahs. He was too smart for that. Abbot ran his hand up and down his left side, over the fist-sized spot of pink-wrinkled flesh where his daddy branded him special. Daddy explained to him how God had commanded him to beat Abbot, and to strike him with the cat-o'-nine-tails as a way to rid him of his sins. He then burned him with the seal of his holy mission—a mission to avenge Adam. Abbot flexed all his muscles and breathed in the sweet scent of the fruit. He would be strong and resist her temptations. It was his sacred duty to put this wickedness to death.

The woman's luscious mouth was moving, drawing Abbot's gaze. She was speaking, but he hadn't heard what she said. "What?"

"I said, I'd be happy to help you pick out some good fruit, if you want. The one you have in your hand is bruised, see?" She touched the soft brown side.

"Thanks." Abbot allowed her to select four apples and set them in his cart before she said goodbye. The woman pushed her buggy through the deli and bakery sections and turned down the cereal aisle. He followed her around the store from a distance and went through the checkout lanes at the same time. He finished first, so he dawdled at the front entrance until the woman came out.

"Hey, thanks again for helping with the apples."

The woman looked startled for a second before she flashed him a come-hither smile. "Sure, good luck." She pushed her cart into the parking lot, and out to her car. Abbot took his bag and ran to his van. He'd have to hurry for his plan to work.

The apples spilled on the floor when he tossed the plastic bag across the bench seat in the cab. He started the engine, not wasting any time in picking up the fallen groceries. The van lurched backward, almost hitting a couple of kids who yelled and flipped him off. Abbot returned the gesture and then raced to the spot where Jezebel awaited him. He squealed to a stop directly behind the woman's car, blocking her in, and opened his door.

The woman narrowed her shifty eyes at him. He'd have to be careful, she was cunning.

She set a grocery sack on the seat in her car and rummaged in her purse. "What do you want?"

The lure. She thinks her trap is about to spring, but she's got it backwards. Abbot glanced around to be sure they were alone before he charged. With both hands, he reached forward, grasping her shoulders and spinning her away from him. He locked her neck in a choke hold and yanked her toward his van. "Your seduction is powerless against me." He spat in her ear.

The woman fought against him, trying to escape. She was strong, but he was bigger. Abbot slid open the door to the back-cargo section of the van and wrestled the temptress inside. He reached for a length of rope with one hand and twisted her arm back with the other. She screamed, the piercing echo shrill inside the contained metal space and through his head. All of a sudden a stream of burning liquid shot into his eyes. An excruciating sting caused him to lose his grip on the woman, and she kicked him in the groin.

Abbot wailed. He rubbed his eyes furiously with one fist, while clutching his crotch with the other. Tears streamed down his face and he couldn't see. His stomach clenched, and he fought against the urge to vomit. The fucking Jezebel was outside screeching, and he knew only one thing.

He had to get away.

Now.

Chapter Twenty-One

Michael called while Kendra was on her morning commute. His voice echoed from her car speakers. "Hey, sis."

"Hey, Michael. You're up early. What's going on?"

"I just got off the phone with Mom. She never remembers I'm two hours earlier than she is."

Kendra laughed. It was six-thirty in the morning, Denver time, and Arizona was an hour earlier still. "What did she need to talk to you about at the crack of dawn?"

"Crack of dawn, nothing. It is still pitch-black outside."

"So? What's going on? Is Dad okay?" Kendra's adopted father had a heart condition. Since her parents rarely called her to chat, she was always on the alert for bad news.

"He's doing fine. No, she called me about you. Said you were thinking of leaving the FBI and might move down here?"

"What?"

"Do you want me to start looking for houses?"

"Oh, my God! I can't believe her! I never said that—or

even anything close to that. That's just what she wants me to do."

Michael laughed. "I figured as much. But Ken, it wouldn't hurt to look at other career options. Ones that aren't so taxing. You could have your own dog training business. I could help you with the business side of things."

Kendra pinned her lips together with her teeth so she wouldn't say what she was thinking. She knew her family was trying to help, in their way. A way that shouted they didn't believe she was up to performing her work either physically or mentally.

"What do you think? I mean, I know this isn't what you were planning, but there really is a house two blocks from mine that just went up for sale. It has a nice yard."

"Michael. I am not leaving the FBI. Why can't you guys get that through your heads?" Frustration gave her tone a sharp edge. "And besides, there are no nice yards in Arizona. They're all rock."

"Whoa. I'm not trying to pressure you. But with Baxter in forced retirement, I thought maybe you'd be thinking of other options too."

"Easier options, you mean?"

"Ken..."

"No. I'll be getting a new K9 partner and going back to my regular job as soon as we solve the serial murderer case."

"Okay, okay. I'm just offering up ideas, that's all."

She sighed. "I know. I appreciate that, but I wish you all would accept that I love being an agent." She pushed her irritation back into its cubby hole deep inside. "Hey, I do have some news though. I'm kind of in a new relationship."

"Oh? Where'd you meet this guy?"

"You know him. It's Rick Sanchez."

"You've got to be kidding. Kendra, he's not the right guy for you."

"Come on, Mike. I thought you liked him."

"He's okay, as far as a guy's guy, but not as someone for you to get crushed by."

Kendra clenched her teeth and sped up into the fast lane. "Why do you automatically assume he's going to crush me?"

Michael paused and softened his tone. "He's not the kind of man who wants to settle down, have a handful of kids and let you train dogs. That's all."

Heat flashed into her face and Kendra almost missed her exit. "I can't believe you! What makes you think that's the type of life I want?"

"Someday you'll realize that living in danger all the time and also loving someone who does, isn't worth it. Don't you want a man you know will come home every night?"

"There's no guarantee any of us will be home every night."

"I'm not just talking about safety. Sanchez strikes me as the kind of guy who likes to live on the edge. There's lots of reasons a man like that doesn't come home at night."

Kendra squealed into the garage and surged into a parking spot. She slammed her car into park. Her breath came fast, and she closed her eyes to calm down. "So, I've had one date and you've got me married with a bunch of kids and a cheating husband? I can't believe you."

"Settle down, Kendra. Just be careful, that's all I'm saying. You really need to think about what you want from life."

She shook her head, her hands still gripping the steering wheel. "Listen, Mike. I'm at work, so I've got to go. In the end, I'm not quitting the FBI or moving to Arizona. All that's on my mind right now is how hot Rick Sanchez would look without his shirt on. So, I think *you* are the one who needs to calm down."

A shadow floated across her window and she glanced out. Rick was standing next to her door leaning on the car parked right beside hers. His smirk told her he heard through the glass exactly what she just said to her brother.

"I didn't call to fight with you, Kendra. I'll talk to you later."

"I know. I'm sorry, I just wish you guys would trust me to decide things for myself. I am a grown woman, you know."

"I never said you weren't."

"Okay, I'll call you later."

She opened her door and looked up at Rick. "So, about that."

"No explanation necessary. I'm just glad to know I'm the only thing on your mind." His laugh was low and sexy. Her body hummed in response, as if he touched her.

"That was my brother. He and my mom are trying to get me to quit my job and move to Arizona."

"Seriously?"

"If you only knew."

CONGREGATED IN THE CONFERENCE ROOM, KENDRA poured over the newest lab reports with the rest of the team. Burke added the names of Tansey's friends to the evidence board along with bullet points from their interview notes, of which there were precious few. No one believed that Tansey Johnson had been murdered. Her few friends said she didn't seem the type to be mixed up in any trouble. Though Kendra knew there wasn't necessarily a type.

Burke interrupted Kendra's concentration. "Lunch is on you today, since you stole the best donut yesterday."

"Whatever, Cameron. Get over it." She laughed. "What are you hungry for?"

"Let's go for Italian. I'll drive, who's coming?"

Rick's eyes narrowed the slightest bit. "I've got a meeting. I'll just get something later."

"We could bring you some food back," Kendra offered.

"That's okay. I'll see you two back here in an hour?"

Kendra smirked. She wasn't sure how she felt about Rick's subtle possessiveness. She nodded and followed Burke toward the elevators.

———

THEY WALKED INTO THE LOBBY OF THE OLIVE GARDEN, and the scent of tangy tomato and Italian spices permeated the air. Burke's stomach rolled in on itself, reminding him how hungry he was. A hostess seated them and Burke opened a menu, though he already knew what he wanted.

"So," he propped his elbow on the table and rested his chin in his hand. "Before we order, tell me what exactly is going on between you and the boss?"

Kendra drew her brows together. "Between me and Oxley?" She pretended she didn't know what he was talking about.

Burke cinched his mouth back on one side and raised an eyebrow to make it clear he didn't fall for her ruse. "No, between you and Sanchez."

"Nothing. What makes you ask?"

"Oh, I don't know. On your first day back it seemed like he was going to ex you out of the investigation—but then he took you with him to the crime scene."

A waitress brought water and took their order. When she left, Burke continued. "Then, Sanchez actually had you physically removed from the next crime scene, and sent you back to headquarters with your tail between your legs."

"He said he was trying to protect me."

"From what?"

Kendra shrugged.

"Well, and then, not twenty-four hours later, it shocked

the hell out of me when the two of you left the bar together."
He shook his head. "And now, this morning, you're both back
to pretending like you hardly notice each other, only the
tension's so thick there's hardly space for the rest of us in the
room. It's damned uncomfortable, that's all I'm saying."

Kendra took a long drink of water, then raised one shoulder. "It's not just uncomfortable... it's complicated."

Burke snorted. "How did I know you were going to say
that?"

"Shut up." She swatted his arm. "I'm serious."

Rolling his eyes skyward, Burke unrolled his silverware
from the napkin. "So, tell me."

"Rick and I met last November when I flew out to Idaho
with Baxter, do you remember?"

"Yeah, when you went to help track down that missing
agent?"

"Yes. The missing agent was Rick's partner."

"So, you saved the day, and now you're Sanchez's hero?"

Kendra laughed. "Hardly. We found the guy, and there
were a few moments of flirting, but it didn't come to anything
before I left to fly back to Denver. I never heard from him, so
I forgot about it."

Their bottomless salad and bread sticks arrived, and they
busied themselves with their first several bites of lunch
before Burke asked her to finish her story.

"The next time I saw Sanchez, he was in my hospital
room when I woke up after being knocked out."

"Nice, and there you were with horrible morning breath."
Burke bunched up his nose and waved his hand in front of his
face. He knew if he kept it light, Kendra would keep talking.

"Right?" Kendra scoffed. "Anyway, then he was around,
coming over every day while I was getting better. There's
definitely an attraction between us. I mean, the guy's hot,
right?"

"Oh, super-hot." Burke smirked and shook his head. "Just the facts, ma'am. I don't need your sexist opinions."

Kendra grinned. "Anyway, he started doing that weird avoiding me thing, so I asked him outright what the hell was going on."

"Good for you." Burke liked that about Kendra. She was a straight shooter and didn't play games.

"Yeah, but I stumbled into some heavy grief. I guess he saw his fiancée murdered right in front of him and now he has serious issues. He's not ready to start anything real. Hell, he might not ever be ready."

"Oh, shit." *Poor guy*.

"Yeah. He's really messed up. I can't even imagine. Of course, he blames himself."

Burke nodded sagely. "So, do you think he's trying to protect you by pushing you away?"

"I do, but I told him that wasn't fair. I'm a fed. This is my job."

"And how do you feel about him? Personally, I mean."

Kendra stared at Burke. He took a big bite of bread and chewed it slowly, letting the buttery garlic swirl around his mouth while he waited for her to answer.

"I'm really drawn to him. I have been from the beginning, in Idaho. We're testing the waters, but I think he's afraid of getting too close."

"Be careful, Dean. You don't want to get hurt either. You know Rick'll be going back to Chicago when we catch our killer." Burke bit into a banana pepper and it squirted Kendra's cheek. He barked a laugh as she wiped off the juice and glared at him.

"I know you're right, but..."

"But... 'he's super-hot'." Burke laughed. "It sounds like the rest of us will just have to put up with it being 'damned uncomfortable' until you two can deal with your hormones."

"Exactly, so shut up and put up." Kendra stuck her tongue out at him and pushed her plate away. She opened the case file she brought with her. The dark eyes of Tansey Johnson stared back at them, demanding they focus on finding her murderer.

———

LATER THAT AFTERNOON, RICK FIELDED A CALL FROM THE local PD. The officer reported a woman escaping an attempted abduction in the parking lot of a grocery store south of Denver, in broad daylight. She could identify her attacker and his vehicle, though she didn't get a license plate number. Rick's pulse skyrocketed.

He leaned out of his office door and called out. "Cameron, can you come in here a sec?"

Kendra stretched back in her chair, peering around the side of her cubicle and smiled at him. Her eyes held question marks and his gut went cold. He returned her smile and winked at her. But when Burke went into his office, he closed the door.

"We may have had a break in the case." Rick took a seat behind his desk and gestured for Burke to sit, too. "I just got a call from the Littleton PD. A man attacked a woman in a King Soopers parking lot. She reports having spoken with the guy inside the store. She's with the department's sketch artist right now, so we should have a description and drawing by this afternoon. She also reported that he was driving a white, cab-forward van with no windows in the back compartment. The bastard tried to shove the woman into the van and tie her up, but she sprayed him with pepper spray, kicked him in the nuts, and got away." He clapped his hands together. "This is our first real break."

Rick tossed the report file on his desk in front of Burke.

He pointed his chin in the file's direction. "I want you to drive out to Littleton and interview the victim. Sounds like she may have just escaped an attack by our guy."

"I hope so. This could be the break we need." Burke sat forward and peered up at Rick. "Don't you want to be the one to talk to her?"

"Yes, damn it." Frustration and excitement warred within him, but Rick trusted Burke to get all the gouge. "Unfortunately, I have an appointment with the ME in half an hour regarding our last victim." Rick straightened his tie and patted his suit-coat pocket. "I'll follow up with her later, but I want someone to talk to her right away, while her memory is fresh."

———

"I'M ON IT." BURKE'S PULSE SPIKED. HE LIKED SANCHEZ, HE seemed like a stand-up guy, but his affinity had more to do with the fact that Sanchez trusted his team, and Burke was a part of that. He pushed his chair back and shoved his arms into his jacket. "Want me to take Dean with me?"

Sanchez met his gaze, but then looked away. "No, you can take Stott if you want, but honestly, I think you can handle this on your own. All I need is the woman's version of what happened and a solid description of her attacker."

Burke pressed his lips together. *Well, he trusts most of his team, anyway.* "No problem."

"I knew I could count on you, Cameron. I'll see you back here at the end of the day."

Burke stood and stretched to his full six foot, two inches. His chest expanded in response to Sanchez's confidence, but he felt bad for Kendra. She was chomping at the bit to be actively involved in this case and this was going to piss her off.

BURKE EXITED RICK'S OFFICE, TRYING TO STIFLE WHAT looked to Kendra like a self-satisfied grin. His expression changed when he saw her. His lips flattened, and he sent her a quick nod before he went to wait for an elevator. *What was that all about?*

Several minutes later, Rick walked out holding a file folder and swinging his suit coat on over his broad shoulders. Shoulders she had run her hands over. The memory evoked a delicious quiver in her belly.

"Where are you headed?" She allowed her gaze to drift down across his chest to his trim waist.

"I've got a meeting with the ME."

"And Cameron? Where did he rush off too?" She lazily scanned the rest of his tantalizing appearance.

Rick hesitated and then slid his suit coat the rest of the way on, tugging to straighten it. "Uh. We got a report this morning about an attempted abduction of a woman at a grocery store."

Kendra sat up, her perusal of Rick cut short by her professional interest. "Attempted?"

"Yeah, the woman got away. She's given a solid description of the guy and of the van he drove away in."

Her pulse bounced like a puppy. "Do you think this is our killer?"

Rick's jaw worked before he nodded, and Kendra realized what was happening.

"Oh—So you sent Cameron out to interview the woman, is that it?"

"Yes." His dark eyes challenged hers.

"I see." She leaned back in her chair and tapped a pencil on the desk. "Good. I get it." She shook her head. "Even after all we talked about the other night... I get it."

"Kendra — "

"Nope, no need to defend your decision. You're the ranking officer. You give the orders." A simmering heat bubbled in her stomach.

Rick shook his head. "Listen, I have to go. We can talk about this later."

Kendra didn't answer. Rick sighed and left the office.

She dropped the pencil and picked up her phone. She swiped the screen and held the device to her ear. It rang three times.

"Federal Bureau of Investigation, K9 Unit. Agent Jennings here."

"Hey, Jennings, it's Dean."

"Hey, how are you? How's the Bax-man?"

Kendra relaxed at the sound of the familiar voice. "I'm good. All better, in fact. Baxter's adjusting to a lazy, comfortable life. Actually, I'm amazed at how quickly he's figuring life out as a tri-pawed."

Clayton Jennings was the lead agent at the FBI K9 Unit in Denver, her immediate supervisor, and a good friend. "Dogs are so freaking awesome. They don't carry any of the baggage humans do, man—they just wake up and face what life brings them that day. I hope you'll bring him in to see us."

"Absolutely, sometime in the next couple of weeks. I will."

"Great! How about you? How's the head?"

"I'm a hundred percent. That's why I'm calling. I'm ready to come back to work."

Jennings hesitated and Kendra heard the familiar sound of dogs barking in the background. "That's good to hear, but I have to get your medical clearance before I can bring you back."

"Don't you have anything over there I could do? Riding the desk here at headquarters is about to drive me crazy." Kendra rolled the pencil under her fingertips and then lifting it started tapping it on the desktop again. "Come on, Clay. I've got to get out of here. They won't let me do anything, so I'm just sitting around. Hell, I'll even clean kennels if I have to."

Jennings laughed. "Okay, why don't you come in tomorrow. We need to start looking into finding you a new partner —I mean, if you think you're ready for that."

A lump formed in Kendra's throat and she nodded. Belatedly realizing Clay couldn't see her, she coughed and swallowed. "Yeah. We should start the process."

"Roger that. Hey, Kendra, don't rush back if you're not ready. That wouldn't be good for you, or a new K9 partner."

"I'm good. See you in the morning." She clicked off. Kendra's greatest worry was how Baxter would feel about having another dog around—one that would occupy a majority of her attention. He didn't deserve that, but what else could she do? She'd have to get another dog if she wanted to remain an FBI K9 handler and get out of this office.

Chapter Twenty-Two

B urke drove to the address of an apartment complex in Highlands Ranch and found the building he searched for. He knocked at number 203 and waited while he listened to footsteps approaching from inside. The door opened about six inches and an attractive woman in her late forties peered out at him.

"Yes? Can I help you?" Her soft southern lilt belied the fierce grip she had on the door.

Burke held up his FBI Badge and ID. "I'm Agent Cameron, ma'am. I'm here to speak with Susan Bell. Is that you?"

The woman hesitated. She studied his ID and then his face, as though trying to decide whether or not to let him in. "No, I'm her mother. Susan's here, but she's resting. It's been an awful day."

"Of course." Burke slid his wallet back into his coat. "I won't take up too much of her time, but it's imperative that I hear her story."

"Who is it, Mamma?" A younger woman's voice sounded from deeper inside.

Without taking her eyes from him, the woman guarding the door called over her shoulder. "It's the FBI. Are you up to talking to an agent right now, sweetheart?"

A young, lithe woman walked up and stood behind the older version of herself, her short blonde hair flipped up in a spunky style.

"Ms. Bell?"

She touched her mother's shoulder and gave her a small smile. "It's okay, Mom."

The mother's brow creased as she considered her daughter. She shrugged and turned to Burke. "Come in, Agent Cameron, but please don't upset her."

"I'm fine, Mamma. Really." Susan opened the door fully and stretched out a hand to shake Burke's. She shook with a firm, confident grip. "Come on in. Agent Cameron, did she say?"

"Yes, ma'am." Burke followed her into the apartment, resolutely not noticing her long legs stretching down from her shorts, and definitely not watching her hips sway.

"Smells good in here." Burke hoped to put the women at ease.

Susan smiled. "Yeah, my mamma's homemade mac and cheese. It's her remedy for all things—comfort food. Would you like something to drink? Iced tea?"

"Sure. Thanks." Burke evaluated the young woman. This was no cowering victim. She seemed strong and self-assured. Susan stepped into the galley kitchen and filled two glasses with ice. She poured dark tea from a pitcher on the counter over the cubes and handed one to Burke.

"Thank you." He sipped and the syrupy flavor surprised him. He licked his lips.

"I should have warned you. It's sweet-tea. Mamma grew up in Georgia."

Burke smiled and walked behind Susan to the living room.

"Have a seat." She gestured to a plaid, overstuffed side-chair. "What can I do for you, Agent Cameron? I already gave the police my statement." She sat on the sofa across from him and tucked her legs up under herself.

"I realize you've already given an official statement to the local PD, but I'd like to hear about what happened in your own voice. Then I have just a few questions. I'll be out of your hair in no time."

She smiled, and it was as if the sun broke through the clouds. Burke felt the warmth on his skin. "It's no problem. Anything I can do to help catch that creep before he tries to kidnap another woman. God only knows what he had in mind."

Burke flipped open a notebook and clicked his pen. "Thank you. That's exactly what we want too. Tell me your account of the incident beginning with your arrival at the grocery store."

Susan unfolded her legs and leaned forward, propping her forearms on her knees. "Well, it was around one o'clock. I parked at the back of the lot because I like to get in extra steps and I hate trying to find an open space."

"Okay. When did you first see the man who attacked you?"

"Not until I was in the produce section. I was picking out apples when this guy pushed his cart up and bumped into me. He was also looking at the apples. I glanced in his cart and saw only junk food." She cocked her head. "You see, I'm a nutritionist... an opinionated one, unfortunately."

Burke raised his eyebrows and smirked. "Okay." He wasn't sure where she was going, but he was content to listen.

"So, I said something about being glad to see that he was at least getting one healthy item. He was buying some fake cheese spread that I'm fairly certain is akin to cancer on a cracker."

"Did he seem angry that you commented on his food choices?"

"No. He stared at me in a kind of blank way and then picked up a badly bruised apple. Obviously, he didn't know how to check his fruit, so I offered to help. I selected four nice apples for him, he thanked me, and I walked away to finish my shopping. I didn't see him again until I was leaving."

"How long was that?"

She shrugged her shoulders. "I don't know, twenty or thirty minutes, I suppose. Then I saw him waiting at the door. He thanked me again, and then I left. I thought nothing of the exchange at all."

"So, when you left the store, you went directly to your car?" Burke drew a quick sketch of the parking lot in his book.

"Yeah. I was setting my last bag into the back seat when a dented white van screeched to a halt behind my car. That alarmed me instantly. I mean white vans are freaky anyway, but this one blocked me in and I couldn't see the rest of the parking lot." Susan rubbed away the goosebumps that popped up on her arms. Her mother rounded the sofa and sat next to her.

Burke pressed on. "Did the man say anything to you at that point?"

"Not right away. I reached into my purse for my pepper spray and asked him if he wanted something." Susan closed her eyes and shivered. Her mother put an arm around her shoulder. "That's when..."

"Take your time." Anger surged through Burke's veins at the idea of this asshole attacking women.

Susan's mother patted her arm and brushed a loose hair from her face. Susan took a couple of sips of her tea. She set the glass on the table and met Burke's eyes. "That's when he attacked me."

He held Susan's gaze. "I know this is difficult, but can you walk me through the attack? Did he say anything? Tell you his plans? Anything like that?"

"He said something about my seduction being powerless against him, or some phrase like that. I don't know what he was talking about. He didn't make sense. Then he tried to force me into the sliding door of the van. He had a rope and was going to tie my hands, but I managed to spray him in the face with my mace. Then I kicked him in the—well, I kicked him in the crotch."

Burke couldn't help the smile that sprang to his lips. "That probably saved your life."

"I don't know. I was so scared. I ran screaming back into the store. Some man called the police. So did the store manager. But by then, the guy was gone."

"Did you see which way he drove? Did he turn right or left?"

Susan shook her head. "No, I'm sorry. All I had on my mind was getting away. Getting to safety. I didn't look back."

Her mother pulled her close and spoke to Burke. "I think the police talked to the man who called them from the parking lot. He said the van raced from the lot, scraping several cars before he flew on to the street, heading south. It's probably in the report."

"Thanks, I'll read through it." Burke turned his attention back to Susan. "Then what happened?"

"An ambulance arrived, and the paramedics checked me out, but other than being scared to death, I was fine. The police took my statement, then my mother came and picked me up, and here I am."

Burke nodded. "Have you talked to a victim's advocate? There are resources available to help you deal with being assaulted."

"I have. Everyone's been great, but I think I'm fine. Mostly, I'm just pissed off."

"I bet." Burke searched her bright blue eyes. "Any flashbacks?"

Susan's shoulders lifted a fraction. "Sometimes. I'm a little worried about trying to sleep." Burke strained to hear her soft answer.

"It's reasonable to expect a few nightmares too. Is it just the two of you staying here?"

Both women nodded.

"I'll see if I can get the local cops to increase their presence on your street, especially at night. I'm sure you're safe. There's no reason at all to believe your attacker knows where you live, but it might help you sleep better knowing the cops are around." Burke figured he'd drive by himself. Her assailant didn't take her purse, but he could have her license plate number. It was always better to be safe than sorry.

Chapter Twenty-Three

Kendra took the first few rich sips of her French-roast morning coffee and watched Baxter totter toward the back door. "What do you think, Bax? Do you want a friend to play with?" She rubbed the top of Baxter's head and squatted down to look in his face. He slopped a wet lick across her cheek. "Good boy. I love you too."

Her chest ached. How could she explain to Baxter that she'd be bringing home another dog? One who would leave with her every morning while Baxter had to stay behind, confined to the backyard in his early retirement? It felt like a betrayal. Kendra couldn't imagine learning to love a different dog the way she did Baxter, but she also knew that a K9 partner had to share all aspects of her life. If she wanted to be on the FBI K9 team, then she had to press forward.

She came out of the bedroom dressed for work in a black T-shirt and cargo pants. Her hair was pinned in a bun above the clasp of an FBI baseball cap. Anticipating his job, Baxter bounced up and down on his hind legs. He used his single front leg to catch himself before the next launch. His excitement was killing her. "You have to stay home today, buddy." She felt like a complete jerk.

He barked, wagging his tail.

Kendra took Baxter to the backyard and tossed his towel-toy for him to retrieve several times before she said goodbye. Kendra cringed at the sound of his whining all the way to her Jeep. With a deep sigh, she started her car and drove down the street, watching Baxter in her rearview mirror, sitting at the gate.

"Good morning, Jennings." Kendra strode into the K9 building, her boots squeaking on the white-speckled tiles.

"Well, look who it is." Clay stood from behind a metal desk and shook her hand. "You're looking better every day. Maybe still a little green around the forehead."

"Yeah, good to know." Kendra pulled the bill of her cap lower. "So, what's the word on getting me a new partner?"

Clay went back to his desk and opened a file. "There are seven sniffer dogs currently in training at Quantico who are ready to go. I wonder if you'd like to fly out there with me and be part of the selection process?"

"Yes, sir. That would be awesome. Thanks." Energy swirled in her belly. Kendra didn't figure she'd get any say in choosing her new dog. She still might not, but being invited to go check out the new trainees was a great opportunity.

Clay grinned at her. "I thought you might be happy about that. We'll fly out tomorrow morning. Until then, I think you said something about cleaning out kennels?"

Kendra smirked at him. "You got it."

"After that, be sure to clear your travel with headquarters, since you are temporarily assigned over there. Do you have someone who can watch Baxter for a couple of days?"

"Yeah, I have a neighbor who loves him. No problem." Kendra went out to the yard to say hello to a few other members of the team before she got busy with her unpleasant chores. It was lunchtime by the time she finished, and she grabbed a burger on her way to the FBI headquarters.

WHEN KENDRA STEPPED OUT OF THE ELEVATOR, SHE noticed Rick wasn't in his office, so she stopped at the reception desk. "Hey, Lucinda. Where is everybody?"

Lucinda continued scribbling something on a hot-pink sticky note before she looked up. "Agents Sanchez and Burke are at lunch."

Kendra nodded. "Okay, well, I need to leave Agent Sanchez a message. Will you tell him I won't be in tomorrow? In fact, I won't be coming into this office anymore. I'll be back over at K9."

That morsel of information seemed to perk Lucinda up. "Oh? We'll miss you." Her voice was sugar-sweet vinegar.

"I'm sure. Well, thanks for doing that. I'll probably see you around."

"Mmm-hmm. Bye." Lucinda wiggled her fingers in farewell.

Kendra kept her eye-roll to herself and went to clear off her desk. She dropped off all of her case work on top of Burke's desk and scribbled him a quick note explaining that she was going to Quantico with Clay and maybe they could get dinner sometime soon.

On her way out, she hesitated at Rick's office door. She opted not to leave him a personal note. He'd get her message from Lucinda and if he wanted to call her, he would.

A UNIT DRIVER PICKED KENDRA AND CLAY UP AFTER THEY landed at Reagan International Airport. Her first step outside smacked Kendra with a brutal reminder of the intense heat and humidity of training in Virginia. It was only spring, but the heat was already oppressive. By the time they got to the car, her blouse was clinging to her skin.

It took almost an hour to drive from DC down to the FBI Training Facility in Quantico. Memories, both good and awful, flooded her mind.

"Hard to believe this is where we met. Lot of water under the bridge since then." Clay spoke while he stared out the window.

The Marine base that housed the FBI Academy was beautiful. Big lush trees lined the drive and old red-brick buildings added to the ambiance. The Marines on this base always seemed sharper than anywhere else in the world. Many were freshly minted butter-bar Lieutenants, locked and cocked. Others were career Marines in Command and Staff. The whole base was green and gorgeous. Well, gorgeous from inside an air-conditioned car. Training in this environment was a matter of surviving in a wild jungle of blood-sucking insects, snakes, and life-threatening heat.

Finally, they arrived at the K9 Training Center at the Academy. She was anxious to meet her new dog. He would come to her fully trained, but she'd need to add the finishing touches. When Kendra went home with a new K9, they would be together 24/7 and would have to learn to trust each other. She knew this was the way, but it was hard to believe she could ever find another dog good enough to replace Baxter as her partner. She filled her lungs with moist air, fragrant with cherry blossoms, and held it for a second before she let it out in a rush. *Well, best get on with it.*

The lead trainer recognized them and approached. "Agents Jennings and Dean. Good to see you." He shook their hands. "We were all sorry to hear about Baxter. How's he doing?"

Kendra's eyes stung, but she blinked the extra moisture away. She was a federal agent, for God's sake. No tears. "He's doing really well. I'm amazed at how fast he's adapted."

The trainer grinned and shook his head. "These dogs, man. They're incredible."

"For sure."

"Ready to check out our new class?"

Kendra shrugged and nodded, not trusting her voice any further. She and Clay followed the man to a long line of kennels. Many of them were empty, their occupants out training in the field.

"When Agent Jennings called, he said you'd be looking for a sniffer dog. The FBI is moving toward Labradors these days."

Clay turned to her. "They've got great noses. Plus, they're the best breed for community relations since they're so social."

The trainer eyed her. "We've got five labs ready to go. One chocolate, one black, and three yellows. We do have a bloodhound, but he's young and won't be through training for a while. So, it all depends on your plans."

Kendra loved bloodhounds, they were the absolute best sniffers with a scent capability of more than a thousand times that of humans. But, she wanted to get back to work, so waiting wasn't an option. "Let's take a look at your labs, then."

The head trainer gave her a sharp nod and spoke into a walky-talky, asking for the dogs to be brought to the yard. "First, I want you to watch them all together at liberty. See what you think. Then we'll do a demonstration. You can work with each dog. Maybe you'll feel a connection."

The pack of dogs barked at each other and cavorted

around the yard, thrilled to be turned out for playtime. After a time, five handlers entered the training area and called the dogs to heel. They demonstrated the dogs' general obedience and discipline before showing off their abilities with different scents and tracking.

After two hours of demonstration, it was time for Kendra to get a hands-on feel for the dogs. She opened the gate and entered the yard. Snapping a tennis ball into a thrower, she tossed the ball, and the dogs raced to it, the winner returning it to her hand for another throw. The heavy weight she'd carried into the academy with her eased. Dogs had a way of helping a person let go of their tension. Before long, Kendra was laughing out loud at their antics.

Separately, she took each dog through a few commands and sent them on an article search. They were all well trained and excited to work, but the lone female, the chocolate lab, seemed to look deep into Kendra's soul. It was as if she could sense the pain that hovered inside. The male dogs were one hundred percent focused on their job. Any one of them would have been a joy to work with, but the chocolate girl was the one. They made an instant connection.

"What's her name?" Kendra knelt down and draped an arm over the dog's shoulders, receiving a love slurp in return.

The trainer patted the dog's head. "This is Annie."

"Annie?" Kendra stroked her face, and the dog rewarded her with a Labrador grin. "That suits you, I think. Would you like to go to work with me, Annie?"

Annie panted, her long pink tongue hanging from the side of her mouth. She licked her chops and worked hard to remain in a sit. Her tail pounded the dirt.

"Okay, let's give each other a try." Kendra stood. "I'll take her. You can work out the details with Agent Jennings."

"Great. After watching you two together, I think you're making the perfect choice."

"Can we take her with us, or will you ship her?"

The trainer checked his clipboard. "We'll send her out to Buckley on the next transport headed that way. Probably a week."

"Sounds good." Kendra said goodbye to Annie, and a handler led the dogs back toward the building. She shook the trainer's hand and she and Clay returned to the car. They would have time to get back to DC before dinner.

———

KENDRA GULPED DOWN AN ICE-COLD, LEMON-LIME Gatorade while she changed her clothes for dinner. Her cell phone buzzed. She saw that it was Rick, and she tapped the screen. "Hey."

"What the hell, Kendra?"

She closed her eyes and drew in a breath. "What's the matter?"

"You just quit the case? You didn't even talk to me about it. I thought we meant more to each other than that. Hell, even if we didn't, you can't just quit without saying anything."

A hot coal flared in her gut. It was just like Rick to only see her part in this. "I did say something. I came in to tell you, but you weren't there, so I left a message with Lucinda. I'm sure she was more than happy to give it to you."

A heavy silence hovered on the line.

Finally, Rick spoke. His voice was low and controlled. "Why?"

"Why did I leave?"

"Yeah, why did you leave, and why didn't you call me?"

Kendra's shoulders drooped. "There was no reason for me to stay. You don't want me on the case, and I'm not somebody who likes to sit around waiting for crumbs. So, I went back to

K9. That's where I work, Rick. You knew I'd be going back there."

"It's not that I don't want you on the case—"

"Yeah, yeah, you're only trying to keep me safe. Whatever. Why didn't you send me with Cameron to interview the woman who escaped the attack?"

Rick was silent again.

"That's what I thought."

"Kendra. I explained."

"Sure, Rick. And I understand your fear, but I can't stop doing my job so you'll feel better. I'm sorry, but I honestly don't see how this is going to work. If it isn't this case, it will be another."

"No, it won't. You don't normally work on serial murder cases. It'll be different."

"Maybe..."

More silence. Kendra crossed the room and stared out the window at the boats on the Potomac.

"When are you coming home?"

"Tomorrow."

"Can I see you?"

"I don't know. It'll be late."

"Come on, Kendra. You're not giving this a chance."

"I'm not the one with the problem."

"Let me take you to dinner tomorrow. We can talk."

Kendra hesitated. She wanted to be with Rick, but her logic argued with her emotions. "I need to get home to Baxter. But, I guess maybe you could come to dinner at my house after work?"

"That'd be great." Rick cleared his throat. "We can work this out, Kendra."

"I hope so."

. . .

KENDRA MET CLAY AND THEY TOOK AN UBER TO AN IRISH Pub in Arlington for dinner. "I think Annie will make a nice addition to the team, don't you?"

"I do. I thought you two worked well together." Clay studied the beer menu.

"Annie did a great job in her searches. She's as good as any bloodhounds I worked with."

"She has a good nose. When she retires, you can take up duck hunting." He laughed and ordered a Murphy's Stout. "How old did they say she was?"

Kendra folded the menu and asked for the same. "Two. She still has a lot of puppy in her, but she's smart."

"Labs are puppies until arthritis sets in. Even then." Clay studied her. "How do you think Baxter will like her?"

Kendra forced out a laugh. "He'll hate her at first. Too much energy." She leaned back in her seat. "He's a good guy though. He'll get used to her, I think." Playing with her fork, she tapped in on the table. "God, Clay. I don't want him to feel discarded. You know?"

"Kendra." He sat forward and braced his forearms on the wood. His short blond hair was tapered up in a high-and-tight reminiscent of his Marine Corps days. "Don't personify him. Dogs aren't like people. They have a pureness to their love. They aren't self-centered like people can be. My money is on him being thrilled to have another lady in the house."

Kendra smiled at him. "I hope so. He doesn't deserve to feel like he's done something wrong when all he did was risk his life to save mine."

Clay nodded then changed his solemn expression in a flash with a wide grin. "What do you want to do tomorrow? Our flight doesn't leave until two o'clock. Want to go to the Smithsonian?"

"Great idea." She'd be glad to have something to do that

would keep her mind off the man waiting for her at home. "Let's go see the changing of the guard at the Tomb of the Unknown Soldier in the morning. I love that."

Chapter Twenty-Four

Rick tracked Kendra and Clay Jennings's flight and saw that it landed just after four o'clock. He wouldn't be able to get away from the office until five-thirty, or so. Sitting with his back to the glorious view of the front range, Rick pulled up the evidence-tracker spreadsheet and timeline. He was settling into a level of deep concentration when his phone buzzed. He glanced at the screen. *Michael?*

"Hey, Michael. What can I do for you?"

"Sanchez, how ya doing?"

Rick tapped his fingers on the edge of the desk. He didn't have time for chitchat today. Not if he was going to get to Kendra's by dinner time. "I'm good, Mike. What's up?"

"I hear things are getting hot and heavy between you and my sister."

Not as hot and heavy as I want them to be. "Where'd you hear that?" He remembered the phone conversation he'd come upon the other day when Kendra was still in her car and his lips eased into a satisfied grin.

"Listen, I know she's a grown woman, but she's still my sister and it's my job to look out for her."

"I'm pretty sure Kendra can look out for herself."

"She doesn't always make the best choices. Take being in the FBI for instance. I mean, I know she's smart, but even you have to admit that isn't the kind of job best suited for her."

"I disagree, Mike. Kendra is a brilliant agent."

"No, no. Like I said, I know she's smart, but it's a dangerous job. You know first-hand what I mean. She has a soft heart and loves dogs like crazy. She'd make a great dog trainer. Don't you think?"

"Kendra would be great at whatever she wanted to do. She would make a great dog trainer, in fact she already is that. She's also an amazing FBI field agent, which is what she wants to do. So..." Rick spun his chair to look out the window. Kendra was sensitive about having to prove herself all the time and the reason was becoming apparent to him in broad strokes. "Anyway, I'm sure you didn't call to discuss how great Kendra is at her job."

"No, you're right. It's just that I thought if you cared for her, then you'd be on board with her moving toward a safer career."

"I do care for her, and in my opinion, that means I want to support her in whatever she wants to do. And right now that means being one of the best agents I know." He spoke the words with authority, but his conscience prodded him with guilt. It was easy to say these words to Mike. It was even easier to judge Kendra's brother for being controlling and overprotective, but those attitudes were exactly what Kendra had been accusing Rick of. He was torn between what he knew was the correct way to see the situation, and the way he actually felt about it. "I understand your concern, though.

Rest assured, I'm doing everything I can to make sure she stays safe."

"She'd be safer if she quit playing cops and robbers."

"That's not what she's doing, Michael, and you know it."

"Well, mostly I wanted to call you and tell you that I'm keeping my eye on you. I may not live close to Kendra, but that doesn't mean I'm not aware of what's going on. You better show her the respect she deserves and don't do anything to hurt her."

Rick smirked at the thought of Michael standing up to him, but even though the guy was half his size, Rick admired his intention. "I think you have the impression that things have progressed between Kendra and me further than they actually have. We're still figuring out if we want to see each other regularly."

"That's not how Kendra views it."

"I think she was just trying to goad you a little." Rick righted his chair and turned toward his desk. This brotherly lecture had gone on long enough. He had to get back to work. "Either way, I hear you. I want you to know I hold Kendra in high regard and would never meaningfully hurt her in any way."

"That's good to hear. You know I'm only a short flight away."

Rick laughed. "Well, to be honest, if Kendra thinks I'm doing anything she deems disrespectful, I have no doubt that she could handle it herself, and probably better than you. So, don't worry."

Michael didn't respond right away. When he did, he sounded miffed. "Consider yourself warned."

"I hear you." Rick shook his head, wishing that he and Kendra's relationship merited the warning.

. . .

After work, Rick drove to Kendra's. The heavy traffic only added to his sense of helplessness and frustration. When he got there, he parked on the street in front of her house. The Explorer's door clicked shut and from his position on the other side of the screen-door, Baxter tossed his floppy ears aside to observe Rick's approach. He barked a loud greeting.

"No bark." Kendra ordered, without conviction from somewhere inside the house. Baxter wagged his tail as Rick walked toward him. He held his hand out for the dog to sniff through the mesh. Kendra smiled tentatively as she crossed the room to open the door. Baxter bounded out to greet him. Together, he and Kendra watched her dog as he tottered around, sniffing the perimeter of the front yard before ambling back up the porch steps to give Kendra a few sloppy licks.

Rick slid his hand over Kendra's, his heart hammering. "Hey, you." He bent down to kiss her cheek, hoping she wouldn't turn away.

"Hi." She peered up at him, her gaze fell to his lips, but instead of kissing him, she turned into the house.

Rick followed. "What's for dinner?"

"I have some chicken breasts in the fridge. How about BBQ, corn-on-the-cob, and some salad?"

"Sounds great. If you want me to, I'll start the grill." They worked together in the kitchen like they'd been cooking side by side for years. The sun hovered above the horizon smearing peach-sherbet swathes across the lengthening evening and the air remained warm. Rick set the table on the back deck while Kendra sprinkled sunflower seeds on the salad.

"Perfect night to eat outside." She pushed through the screen door carrying a bowl in one hand and balancing two beers in a stranglehold around their bottle necks in the other.

"Thanks for having me." He let his gaze wander over her figure. He anticipated what might be for dessert if tonight went well. Of course, that was a big 'if'. "The chicken is just about ready."

She set the salad and bottles on the table and took her seat. She dished the greens onto their plates and glanced over at him.

"I haven't taken the time to relax and watch the sun set in so long I can't remember. Your view is incredible." Rick rested back and crossed an ankle over his knee.

"Colorado sunsets are spectacular."

Rick nodded and sipped his beer. "Your brother called me today."

"Michael? What for?"

"I think he wanted to give me the 'big brother's watching' lecture." He chuckled but cut his mirth short when he saw Kendra's expression. She looked pissed.

"Oh, my God. I'm twenty-eight years old. I can't believe he would do that."

"Don't be mad at him. He's just being a guy. I respect it. If I had a sister, I'd probably do the same thing."

Kendra glared at him. "You probably would. I suppose he told you to fire me too, or something like that."

A warning bell went off in his head. Rick didn't know why her irritation was suddenly aimed at him, but it was. "No, he's just concerned about you. He loves you, is all."

"I know he loves me, he just doesn't believe I can think for myself or keep myself safe."

Rick shrugged and hoped that if he stayed silent, the mood would blow over.

Kendra sat down and tipped the beer bottle to her mouth. "Listen, I'm not very good at pretending like everything is fine, when it isn't."

"Okay, so let's talk." His chest compressed and made

breathing uncomfortable. He sat forward and rested his forearms on the table.

Kendra's eyes hardened. "First, tell me how things went with Cameron's interview."

Rick took a swig of beer, the bitter hops biting his tongue. "The woman he interviewed was attacked in a grocery store parking lot. The guy tried to wrestle her into his van but she sprayed him with pepper spray. She escaped from him, but he sped away before the police got there."

"You think the man who attacked her is your killer, don't you?"

Rick bought a few seconds by twisting his fork in his salad. "Yeah, I think he might be. If so, this would be the first real break we've had in the case. The woman sat with the sketch artist and was able to give a thorough description."

Kendra leveled her gaze at him for an uncomfortable minute and Rick tried to act like he didn't notice. He stood to remove the chicken from the grill and set it on their plates.

"Any particular reason you didn't send me with Cameron that day?"

Rick shrugged. "He asked if I wanted him to take Stott, but I told him I thought he could handle it on his own."

Her eyes didn't move, and she blinked them in a slow, considering sort of way that had sweat beading along the back of his neck. "So, why didn't you ask *me* to go? I was sitting right next to Burke."

"Kendra, come on." His voice was louder than he intended, and her brows shot up. He softened his tone. "Why are you being so sensitive? If it were anyone besides me giving the orders, would you even notice?"

Her brows gathered and she narrowed her eyes. "I could ask you the same thing. If it were a different agent sitting there, would you have included them?" Kendra pushed away from the table and stood. "I just can't tell if you think you need to protect me, or if you truly believe I can't handle my job. Either way, it pisses me off."

"You're too close to this case. You're too emotional. Just like now." Rick swallowed against the rise of angry defensiveness surging up his throat.

Kendra glared at him. "I'm not being emotional. I'm standing up for myself. I'm a good agent. I'm just as good, if not better than Agent Cameron. Damn it, Rick! What do I have to do to prove myself to you? I swear, you're no different than Michael or even my parents, for that matter." She snatched up her plate and marched inside, practically tossing it onto the counter next to the sink.

Rick followed her. "This is what you call *not* being emotional?" Heat bloomed full in his chest now. *God, I can't win.*

She spun around to face him. "I am sick and tired of having to try so hard to prove myself and still not getting to do the work I'm good at. And if you won't let me do my job, how will I ever prove that I can?"

"It was just an ordinary interview. Why are you so mad? I think you're looking for an offense where none was intended." Rick crossed his arms over his chest and met her glare with one of his own.

"*You* said you think I'm too close to this case. So don't pretend now that you're not trying to keep me away from it." Baxter moved from his bed to Kendra's feet. He barked one loud warning at Rick.

Tension bunched in his jaw. He was only trying to protect Kendra, but she obviously didn't appreciate it. How could she not understand? He'd told her about Alyssa being killed right in front of him. He couldn't let that happen again. Now, everything was a big mess. "For God's sake, Kendra, I'm sorry. But there's no reason for you to get in such a tizzy. Cameron and Stott interviewed Lisa Rector's husband. It just made sense for them to interview this woman too."

Kendra shook her head, her face screwed up into angry frustration. "I am *not* in a tizzy." She mirrored Rick's stance by crossing her arms. "You know what? It's probably time for you to go."

Cold water tossed in his face wouldn't have shocked him more. "Kendra..."

"I'm serious." She marched toward the front door and held it open.

Rick choked back bitter words and a self-protective fury wrapped around his shoulders. He didn't need this. What had he been thinking? Relationships took too much effort and caused too much pain. "You're right. I'm out." Rick grabbed his car keys from the counter and stalked out the front door. He sat in his car until the adrenaline from his anger ebbed. Ignoring the urging from his heart to swallow his pride and go back inside, he rammed his car into drive and sped away. Vulnerability was overrated.

———

KENDRA CLAMPED HER MOUTH SHUT, ANGRY AT HERSELF for sending him away, but unable to say anything to stop him. *Shit.* A little over forty-eight hours ago, she had confessed to Rick that she always felt less than—felt like she had to work twice as hard to prove her competency in a man's world. The very next day, he had the gall to ignore her availability and send Burke—a man, and a junior agent to boot—to do an interview. *An interview! Rick thinks he needs to protect me from doing an interview? How pathetic does he think I am?*

She dumped her chicken breast into Baxter's bowl. *Someone should enjoy this.* Kendra marched out to the deck to collect the rest of the dinner dishes. She covered her face with her hands, fighting back angry tears and instead let out a loud growl of frustration. Gradually, her anger lost its heat, and her chest ached. *It's better this way,* she told herself. *When this case is solved, Rick will be going back to Chicago, anyway. Easier to put a stop to things now.*

After the dishes were all washed and put away, Kendra sat on her couch with the beer Rick only drank half of. Thoughts of his lips on the bottle stabbed at her already sore heart. She'd had high hopes for their evening together, but then she made a mess of everything. Baxter rested his jowls on her knee and looked mournfully up at her out of the top of his bloodshot eye sockets.

"I know. I'm an idiot. Stop looking at me like that." She leaned forward and kissed his cold, wet nose. "You believe in me, don't you Bax?"

Her dog slurped his tongue across her cheek. His breath smelled of BBQ sauce. Kendra held his face in her hands. "Maybe I need to stop caring so much about what other people think."

Baxter's tail thumped against the floor.

Chapter Twenty-Five

Rick drove too fast, trying to escape his sense of loss and failure. He knew better. He never should have started something with Kendra. She deserved more than he could give, not to mention she was a co-worker. Relationships didn't belong at work. It never went well.

He pressed the accelerator and felt the turbo kick in. The temporary feeling of power would be worth the ticket if he got pulled over. Rick hated being at the mercy of things beyond his control. The only way to keep Kendra safe was to keep her away from the investigation. He regretted that she thought he didn't believe in her. That wasn't true. He knew her to be a smart, intuitive, and highly competent field agent. In fact, Rick had been happy to have Kendra on the case at first.

It wasn't about that. It was about the gritty, twisting feeling in his gut that the murderer had somehow fixated on Kendra. Rick had no facts to back up his premonition. There was only what could be easily passed off as a coincidence. But three murdered women, all in Kendra's neck of the woods, by a killer who up to this point never killed in the same place twice—was too much. He could be wrong, but it wasn't worth the risk.

Rick grudgingly admitted to himself that his feelings for Kendra were getting in the way of him viewing the case from a purely professional perspective. Another reason to step away from thoughts of having a romantic relationship with her. What he needed was to go meet some random women and get his mind off work, and especially off Kendra.

He parked in his apartment's garage and walked straight across the street to the local watering hole. Two attractive women sitting together at the bar smiled at him as he approached. This was so much easier than caring. He ordered bourbon with a beer chaser. When it came, he tossed back the whiskey, enjoying the burn before he raised his pint glass toward the women along with his best "come get me" smile.

They giggled, and the brunette waved. Rick winked back and paid for their next round of drinks. He felt old and tired going through the motions of flirting with strangers in a bar. The ladies brought their cocktails—sweet frothy confections of some kind—to his side of the counter and suggested moving to a table. A blend of their spicy perfumes swirled around him. They told him their names, but he wasn't really listening. Coming here had been a mistake. He thought about calling Kendra—trying once again to explain—but he knew it wouldn't do any good.

A hand clasped his bicep which automatically flexed at the pressure.

"Oooooh." The woman exclaimed. "Cindy, check out these muscles."

Rick closed his eyes to cover the roll. The game was so inane. "Do you ladies live around here?"

"Close enough." Cindy giggled.

They sat at a table, with Rick in the middle, and shared vague details about where they lived and what they did for a living. A chilly breeze cooled the air when the front door opened to a woman with long blonde waves. An hour-glass figure, heavy on the topside swayed into the bar. Searching the room, the woman turned and saw her friends—the ladies Rick was sitting with. They all cooed and waved at each other.

Lucinda. Shit.

"Well, what a surprise to see you here, Agent Sanchez," she purred. "How do you all know each other?"

The brunette clung to the arm she'd been feeling up. "You know Rick?"

Lucinda's smile slid onto her bright red lips. "I do. In fact, we work together, don't we... *Rick?*"

He studied her perfect makeup, her lush long hair, and her curves. She really was hot. Lucinda had made her availability known to him every day since he first came to Denver. Honestly, she was exactly the type of woman Rick could lose himself in for several hours of meaningless escape. He probably would have done so by now if he wasn't tied up in knots over Kendra. "That's true. You ladies are all friends?" He forced a chuckle. "How lucky can one guy get?" The words tasted like drywall spackle.

Lucinda's friends tittered, but she stared straight into him with fire in her eyes. "A guy like you? I imagine he could get pretty lucky." She ran her tongue across her lower lip.

Some magical feminine communication happened that he was unaware of, but the results were clear. The brunette excused herself to use "the ladies" and Lucinda ended up snuggled up to him, practically in his lap. Her jasmine scent inundated him. Shots arrived at the table and a quiet warning bell went off in Rick's head. If he took the shot, he knew it was the beginning of something he might not be able to stop.

"Cheers."

Three shots and two beers later, Rick sifted through his

thickened thoughts to remember why it wasn't a good idea to leave the bar with these ladies. They were sexy and funny, they wanted him, and he wanted to distract himself, but... Kendra.

Shit. Rick forced his lips into a smile. "Listen, ladies. Thanks for drinking with me. It's been fun, but I've got to go." He stood in the puddle of their pleas for him to stay. "I'm sorry. Have a good night and Uber home safely."

He pulled out his wallet on the way to the bar and dropped three twenties on the counter. "For their next round, and keep the change." The bar tender nodded, and Rick left the pub. He stood, taking a deep breath of the cool, crisp air, and tried to shake off his buzz. He wasn't ready to go home, so he walked down the street lined with shops that were all closed for the evening.

"Rick," a woman's voice called his name. "Wait."

He turned to see Lucinda tapping toward him in her impossibly high heels.

"Lucinda, you should head back to the bar with your friends." He jammed his hands into his pants pockets.

She slid her hand under his arm and pressed against him. "I'd rather be with you."

"That's not going to happen." He took a step back. "We had fun tonight, but that's where it ends. We work together. It's not a good idea."

She gave him a pretty pout and then touched his lips with her finger. "You and Agent Dean work together too, but I see the way you look at her. If she were here, I bet you'd take *her* home."

Rick closed his eyes and rode the emotional wave that rolled through him at her words. She was right. If it were up to him, he'd have taken Kendra home the other night. Now it was too late. "Listen, Lucinda. You're a beautiful woman, but I've got a lot on my mind. I need to be by myself tonight." He pulled her hand away from his arm. "I'll watch 'til you get back to the bar."

"You're sure? It wouldn't have to mean anything beyond tonight."

"I'm sure."

Lucinda sighed. "Can't blame a girl for trying."

"It's a compliment. I'm just not the right guy." *But am I crazy? It's not like Kendra wants anything to do with me.*

"I guess I'll see you at the office, then?"

"Yeah. You girls get home safe."

"We will." She rushed to him, grabbed his lapels, and kissed him hard. "You too." She tucked a slip of paper into his hand. "In case you change your mind. Call anytime. It doesn't matter how late."

His pulse rocketed and desire that was pure lust beat a tattoo. He sucked in a gulp of air and took two steps back. Rick stared at Lucinda as she turned and hurried back to the bar.

What a mess. He couldn't move forward and didn't want to go backward. Rick picked up a small stone and threw it as hard as he could.

Women.

Chapter Twenty-Six

A bbot wiped his face with a cold cloth. The skin around his eyes still burned. He had somehow found his way back to his motel after the grocery store fiasco. It had been nearly impossible to drive with his eyes streaming from the pepper spray that bitch hit him with. It was lucky no one had followed him because he wouldn't have been able to tell if they did. It was hard enough to see the road in front of him. It took two days before his eyes stopped watering constantly. The lady from the market would get hers, but first, he had something more important to attend to.

In one more hour, he would implement his plan to snatch that female FBI agent. *Kendra Dean*. Once Abbot had come across the news article that included her name, he searched and searched for her address, but in the end, all he could come up with was a post office box. But that was enough. The mail box was located in the Sedalia Post Office. He looked it up in Google maps on the computer and wrote down the directions.

All he had to do now was watch and wait. He had enough food to last at least twenty-four hours. She'd show up to collect her mail eventually, and then he'd follow her home. It was the perfect plan.

The sun finally gave up the day and Abbot took his bag of snacks and drove to the main street in Sedalia. He parked his van in a dirt parking lot directly across from the post office. Slouching down in the seat, he settled in to wait for his prey.

The dark-haired vixen that haunted his dreams hadn't turned up before the post office closed. Abbot watched the postal employees leave, locking the doors to their half of the building. The long, glassed-in hallway that housed the rented mail boxes remained unlocked and an occasional person arrived throughout the evening to collect their post. Nine o'clock came and went and still no Kendra Dean, but Abbot was prepared to wait as long as it took.

He tore open the bag of pretzels and popped the jar of Cheez Whiz. He dipped into the tangy spread and thought of his experience with the daughter of Eve at the grocery store several days ago. He'd been taught how Eve had tricked Adam into eating the forbidden fruit and ruining life for the rest of humanity forever. Abbot was made to understand the treachery of women, and if he ever questioned the lesson, it was beaten into him again so he would never forget.

Secretly—certainly not openly—lest he get the whip to his back and ass, Abbot had always thought Adam was a bit of a pussy to fall for Eve's lies. But instead of proving what an idiot Adam was, what happened to Abbot that day, right in the middle of the grocery store, showed just how crafty Eve could be.

Abbot had picked a perfectly fine piece of fruit for himself, but in seconds a seductress was upon him, offering him not one, but four apples of her own choosing. Abbot found himself momentarily helpless, and he took the fruit. He'd even purchased it before he fully realized the trap. Blue-hot heat radiated up from his gut and simmered behind his eyes when he remembered how he had tried to make her pay, but she got away from him.

He closed his lids over his still sensitive eyes. He wasn't done with her yet. That harlot would pay for what she did. Abbot would prevent her from plying her treachery to other men. But first, he had to silence the siren song that came to him day and night, hauntingly sung to him by the image of Kendra Dean.

Well past nine o'clock, a red Jeep Renegade pulled into the post office parking lot. The headlights clicked off and Abbot's pulse turned on. His breath caught as he waited for the door to open.

He'd been waiting for over three hours. There was no guarantee that this was Agent Dean come to collect her mail today, but he stared at the car, hoping. The door opened, and one booted foot touched the ground. The windows were tinted and he couldn't see the owner of the leg. His heart tapped like a marimba along his ribcage.

A second boot hit the ground but the upper-body was bent into the Jeep. Abbot's leg bounced with nerves and he wiped his hand across his face, peering into the night. The body shifted and arms lowered a dog to the pavement—a three-legged dog.

It's her!

KENDRA SCRATCHED BAXTER BEHIND ONE OF HIS FLOPPY ears. "Good boy. Let's go get the mail." No one was around at this time of night, so she didn't bother with his leash. They walked together into the post office and found her box. Two bills and three political fliers were rubber banded inside a passel of ads. Kendra stood next to a large trash can and dumped each envelope in, one by one, except for the bills.

"Nothing good, Bax. As usual." The dog sat at her feet peering up at her. She smiled and rubbed his head. "Come on, goofy. Let's go home." Kendra opened the door for Baxter.

She stepped out behind him on the concrete landing and froze. Her gaze scanned the surrounding area. There was something. Hairs on the back of her neck stood up and an icy finger trailed a jagged path down her spine. Kendra's stomach clamped down and her breath went shallow. Baxter sensed the change in her and sniffed the air. He licked his jowls and whined.

"What is it, boy?" Kendra shuddered. She squeezed her new Sig in its shoulder holster at her side with her arm to reassure herself of its presence. "Let's get out of here." All senses on high alert, Kendra made her way to the Jeep. Keeping her back to the vehicle as best she could, she hoisted her dog inside. She glanced in the back seat before she stepped into her car and flipped the lock. Safely inside, Kendra scanned the area thoroughly, once again. She didn't see anything unusual, nothing that should give her the heebie-jeebies.

"I'm just freaking myself out, aren't I Bax?" Kendra started her car and clicked on the seat heater to chase off her chill. "I'm letting Rick's paranoia get to me. Let's get home." Baxter curled up on the seat and she pointed her jeep southbound, out of the small town. Thoughts of Rick and how they ended things earlier sat like a twenty-pound stone in her gut. She wanted to call him, but he was so angry when he left, it would be better to wait and talk to him in person.

Behind her, headlights flashed on and then abruptly

snapped off. She stared into her rearview mirror but no cars were there. It was probably her own reflection in the glass of the post office. Her imagination needed to give her a frickin' break.

Chapter Twenty-Seven

✿

I t was after hours, but Burke rationalized that federal
agents didn't keep regular hours. He convinced himself,
as he drove across town to Susan Bell's apartment
complex, that he was only going a little above and beyond in
his quest to keep the community safe. At first, he intended to
do a simple drive-by, but when he thought of Susan's plucky
curls and her determined chin, he changed his mind and
parked his car.

"Agent Cameron? Is everything all right?" Big blue eyes
stared at him through the cracked open door. She opened it
wider. "Come in."

"Thanks." He entered. "Sorry it's so late. Are you here
alone? Where's your mother?" Burke glanced around the
small space.

Susan closed and locked the door before facing him. "I
sent my mother home." She grimaced. "She was driving me
crazy."

"Is there anyone else who can stay with you? Or maybe
you could go to a friend's?"

"Why, did something happen?"

He hadn't meant to frighten her. "No, nothing has happened, but I don't like the thought of you here alone after being attacked."

Her shoulders relaxed. "I'm sure I'll be fine. That creep has no idea who I am, or how to find me."

Burke scratched his chin. "How are you doing? Have you been feeling afraid or depressed?"

"Not depressed, but I have to admit it is upsetting to think about how close I came to being kidnapped." Susan tugged at the hem of her shirt. "Do you think he's the guy who murdered those three other women I heard about in the news?"

"It's a good possibility. We're grateful to have the sketch you helped the police artist with. And it really helps to know the type of vehicle he was driving too."

"I'm sorry I didn't get the license plate number." She wrapped her arms around herself and squeezed tight.

Burke stepped toward her and reached out to touch her arm. "Don't be. You're home tonight—alive, and safe. That's all that matters. You've been a tremendous help in the investigation. I can't believe how brave you were."

She smiled up at him. "You really think so?"

"Yeah, I do. You were prepared, you kept your head, and followed through with your pepper spray. I'm impressed." Burke smiled at the pink flush that filled her pale cheeks. His fingers itched to brush across her skin, so he turned away and took a few steps to distance himself.

"I've carried pepper spray in my purse since I was a teenager. It's funny, I've often wondered what I would do if someone ever tried to attack me. You know? I mean, would I think clearly and take the right steps or would I panic and fall apart?"

"Seems like you stayed focused."

"Kind of. I feel like I panicked and only somehow

managed to use the mace. When I look back, it doesn't seem clear at all. There are single snapshots of actions in my mind rather than a reel of the whole event."

"That's normal. Our brains are phenomenal at protecting our emotional side. You'll probably remember more with time and distance—when you're ready to deal with it."

"I suppose." Susan gestured toward the couch. "Would you like to have a seat, Agent Cameron?"

"You can call me Burke." He lowered himself onto the cushion wondering what made him say that.

She smiled. "Can I get you something to drink, Burke? Or maybe you're hungry? I was getting ready to heat up some left-over chicken and rice for dinner. It's not fancy, but it will fill you up."

Burke's stomach growled, and they both laughed. "Sure, that sounds great, if it's no trouble. What can I do to help?"

Susan walked to the kitchen, her bare red-tipped toes peeking out from under the hem of her jeans. She opened the refrigerator. "Why don't you tear up some lettuce for a salad. Everything is in the veggie drawers." She pulled out a covered casserole dish and set it on the stove.

A set of knives sat behind a cutting board on the counter, and Burke got to work chopping vegetables. Susan plated two servings of the meat dish and heated them in the microwave, filling the tiny kitchen with the scent of roasted chicken and cheese.

After a companionable dinner on the couch, the two watched sitcoms on the TV while sharing a large, dark-chocolate brownie with vanilla ice-cream for dessert.

"Hey, Burke." Susan licked her spoon.

He met her gaze wondering if she felt as comfortable as he did. "Yeah?"

"Thanks for hanging out with me tonight. I suspect babysitting isn't part of your job description, but I was more nervous than I admitted. You being here has really helped."

He grinned. "I aim to serve." Burke wanted to spend more time with Susan, but she was the victim of a crime he was investigating, and that meant tangling with too many ethical violations. "I should be going." He took his dishes to the sink. "I'll make sure there's a patrol car posted out front all night. You won't have to feel afraid."

Susan followed him into the kitchen and stood facing him, blocking his path to the front door. "You're very thoughtful."

"Just doing my job." His blood thickened, and he reminded himself to stay in check.

She pressed her hand against his chest. "Don't go yet. I want to say... well, I'd like to see you again."

Her touch burned through his shirt, and he closed his eyes briefly. Burke clenched his jaw and shifted his weight backward. She stared into his face, expectantly.

He cleared his throat. "I'd like that too, but we'll have to wait until this case is closed."

Burke stepped back, mostly so he wouldn't be an idiot and pull her into his arms. Reaching into his hip pocket, he pulled out his wallet. "Here's my card. If you've got a pen, I'll write my personal cell number on the back."

Susan went to search for something to write with, and Burke headed toward the door. After writing his number down, he turned the knob. "Even though there's a cop watching your place, be sure to lock both locks after I leave."

She smiled and reached up to his shoulder. On tip toes, she stretched up and kissed his cheek, lingering long enough that he couldn't resist. He turned and kissed her mouth, but when her other arm lifted toward his neck, he grasped both of her wrists. "God, you're making this hard." He grinned and brought her hands down between them. "Call me if you need anything at all, and hold on to that card. I'm certain we'll have this guy locked up in the next couple of weeks. Then..."

"Okay—I can see that you're a boy scout. Which is actually really nice. Unusual in today's day and age." Her soft pink lips curved into a smile.

"When this is all over, I'll have to see what I can do to change that image." He pressed a quick kiss on her cheek and left, closing the door firmly behind him, before he could change his mind.

Chapter Twenty-Eight

❦

Kendra turned into her driveway and helped Baxter navigate his way out of the Jeep. She walked to the porch and sat in the dark on the bench-swing, waiting for Baxter to take care of business before they went inside for the night. Her heart was heavy. With distance, she regretted her behavior toward Rick earlier. So many times, he tried to reassure her that he thought she was a smart and competent agent. She was the one who had a hard time believing he meant it.

In truth, she realized he was over protective, not because he didn't believe in her, but because his fiancée had been killed right before his eyes. It made perfect sense that he would never want to go through anything like that again. But, and this was a big but, his fiancée had been a civilian. Kendra was an FBI field agent. Huge difference.

Baxter growled and dashed into the shrubs between her house and the neighbors. He was probably chasing their old cat again. Kendra stood and paced across her porch. "Hurry up, Bax." Frustration welled up in her chest. She was mad at

Rick but even more angry with herself. "Baxter!" *Where did he run off to?*

It wasn't unusual for Baxter to wander off, following his nose. But he hadn't done that since his surgery, and he always came when she called him, if he was close enough to hear. Kendra shrugged and unlocked her front door. *I guess he'll come back when he's good and ready, or when that cat swipes her claws across his nose.*

ABBOT FOLLOWED HER WITH HIS LIGHTS OFF, FROM AS FAR back as he could without losing her altogether. Her house wasn't far from the post office. Not more than four miles. When she turned onto her road, he slowed down to a crawl. He watched her pull into a driveway three houses down from the corner.

Abbot slowed and squared the block, parking the next street over. With his headlights off, he glided to a stop at the far end of her block. The houses were each on a full acre or more which would come in handy if she screamed. He watched Kendra go up her steps and sit on her porch in the dark, waiting for her dog.

That damn dog. He'd caused trouble before. Abbot considered what to do about the bloodhound. He didn't want him barking and alerting his master. She'd be hard enough to handle *without* any warning. Abbot got out of the cab and crawled into the back of the van to get his bottle of Rohypnol tablets. He carried both pills, and a filled syringe. If it worked on women, it would work on a dog. Abbot covered a pill in a dollop of Cheeze Whiz. Easy.

KENDRA FLIPPED ON A LAMP IN THE LIVING ROOM NEXT TO the sofa and tossed her bills on the end table. She turned on the news and fished a beer out of the fridge. The memory of Rick drinking a beer in her kitchen flooded her mind. Once again, she considered calling him to apologize. But it was late. She'd see him tomorrow. Kendra took a long drink of her stout.

She and Rick never did eat their dinner and her stomach complained about its emptiness. On her way out of the kitchen, Kendra grabbed a bag of potato chips. She flopped onto the couch to watch TV and munched on her salty, late-night snack.

THE DOG WAS DOWN. THE DOSE WAS LARGE ENOUGH TO knock out a full-grown woman. Who knew what it would do to a dog, but he'd definitely have the time he needed. Abbot skirted the yard staying along the line of the bushes. She didn't have any of her drapes or shades closed, so he could see her clearly in the light of her living room. Unsuspecting of what awaited her, she carelessly watched her TV show. A slow grin spread across Abbot's face.

Remaining in the shadows, his gaze moved over her form. His breath came fast when she licked salt from her fingers. His body stiffened and a heady urgency coursed through his groin.

KENDRA POLISHED OFF THE REMAINS OF THE CHIPS AND took the bag to the trash. On her way to the kitchen, she looked out the front window. When she didn't see Baxter, she shook her head and strode to the back door. The old door stuck, and she pulled hard to open it. Leaning on the screen door, she held it ajar. "Baxter. Baxter, come!" Listening hard for signs of her dog, she peered into the darkness. "Where the hell are you Bax? Come on!"

She waited a few minutes before giving up, but she left the door open so she could hear him when he came home. Kendra walked down the hall to her bedroom and turned on the light. Removing her shoulder holster, she laid her gun on her nightstand, then she pulled off her top on her way to the bathroom. Her toe rammed into the door frame when she kicked off her slacks. "Shit!" Hopping on her injured foot, she crossed the room to her bed to inspect her stubbed toe. Kendra had split her toenail and blood seeped around the edge. She limped on her heel to find a bandage.

A noise sounded from out in the yard and Kendra hurried to doctor her toe. "Coming, Bax. Hold on." Taking a floral silk robe down from the hook on her bathroom door, she slid her arms into the sleeves on her way out to the kitchen. But Baxter wasn't waiting at the door when she got there. She opened the screen and called out. "Baxter, come on. I want to go to bed." *Where the hell is he now? He was just here.*

THE LIGHT WENT ON IN A BACK ROOM AND ABBOT adjusted his position so he could spy on Kendra there. He watched as she pulled her T-shirt up over her head revealing a lean torso. The sight of her breasts encased in black lace caused him to gasp. He reached for himself, rubbing to ease the ache. *Bitch. Look what you're making me do.* Abbot knew that touching himself was a terrible sin. His daddy caught him at it once when he was thirteen and beat him so badly he missed school for a week.

He remembered Daddy cradling his head as Abbot fought for consciousness and crying. "Don't you see, son. This is what women do to you. They lead you down paths of sin and death. You must be strong. They use your urges against you, and when they get you under their wicked spell, they take everything you have and leave you for dead. I have to teach you. You understand, don't you? Abbot?"

Abbot's mother disappeared when he was young. Since then, until he died several years ago, his daddy worked hard to teach him how to please God. When he was old enough, Abbot left home. He quickly learned that Daddy had been right. Women caused men to sin and separated them from God. He had to stop that from happening to him. He would make up for what Adam, the first man of creation, lost. Maybe then, God would give him relief from his sinful desires.

He stared glassy-eyed at the woman as she took off her pants, displaying lacy panties that matched her bra. She stubbed her toe and hopped to the bed. His hand moved faster until he couldn't hold back a groan. She sat up, suddenly still—listening. *Damnation! She'd heard him in his disgrace.* Humiliation and fury swelled in his throat. Shame draped over him like a shroud.

The woman finally covered herself in a robe, and made her way to the back door. Abbot pressed back into the hedge, further from the pool of light. She called out to her dog. *Good luck with that.* He smirked.

———

KENDRA YANKED OPEN THE UTILITY DRAWER IN THE kitchen and rummaged for a flashlight. She slid her feet into her Uggs and stepped out on the back deck. She aimed the beam out into the yard. "Baxter, come!" Slower now, she edged the light along the line of shrubbery. A breeze picked up causing the branches to sway. "Bax, if you don't come soon, you'll have to sleep outside."

Frustrated, she stalked into the living room to watch the rest of Jimmy Kimmel. If Baxter didn't come back by the time the show was over, she was going to bed. His kennel gate was open, so he could sleep in his doghouse. It was what he deserved for not coming when she called.

———

AFTER MURMURING A PRAYER ASKING FOR FORGIVENESS FOR what the woman caused him to do, Abbot made his way to the breaker box on the side of the house. Kendra Dean would pay for forcing him to embarrass himself before God. He threw the main switch. All the lights flicked off, and a current coursed through his own nervous system in anticipation.

———

NEAR THE END OF THE MONOLOGUE, THE ELECTRICITY clicked off and the canned laughter went silent. Kendra sat up, disoriented, for several seconds in complete darkness. *What the hell?* She felt her way back to the kitchen to get the flashlight she'd left by the toaster, but it wasn't there. Her fingers searched the top of the counter. *That's strange. I just had it.* After feeling around for the battery-operated light and finding nothing, she went in search of her phone.

Kendra crept along the hallway, trailing her fingers along the wall to guide her on the way to her bedroom. She was fairly certain that her phone had been in her pants pocket, or maybe her purse. *Where did I leave my purse?* On hands and knees, Kendra felt around on the floor. Her toe throbbed from being dragged behind her. When she found her slacks, she patted them up and down, feeling for her phone, but there was only fabric. She sighed and sat back against her bed. *Shit. I bet it's in the car.*

The screen door creaked and then slammed shut. Kendra's blood turned to ice water and needles shot through her skull. *Someone's in the house!*

After the initial rush of terror, a cold clarity settled over Kendra's shoulders. On hands and knees, as silent as possible, she crawled to the nightstand where she left her gun. She forced Baxter, and what might have happened to him, out of her thoughts. *Focus.*

Kendra wedged herself into the corner of the room next to the bedside table and waited. She slowed her breathing and listened. If the intruder came through the door, she'd see him first. The darkness helped as much as it hindered. Silently, air passed in and out of her lungs, but her heart slammed against her ribs like a jackhammer. It was difficult for her to hear anything else. Still she waited.

Sweat slicked her palms making her weapon hard to grip. One at a time, she wiped her hands on the carpet. She listened.

No sound came from the front room. No footsteps crept down the hallway. Kendra considered the noise she heard at the back door. Maybe she hadn't latched it and the wind caught it and slammed it shut. She waited a little longer. Laughing at herself for over reacting again, Kendra relaxed her tense muscles and crawled out of her hiding spot. *I have Rick to thank for this paranoia.* She smirked and set her pistol back on top of the nightstand, feeling the slick side of her phone against her pinky. *Oh, brother. As soon as I settle down, I find it. Of course.*

Her silk robe had loosened in her rush to hide, so she adjusted it and tightened the belt. She sat on the edge of the bed and slid her thumb up the phone screen to the utility options. A bright light shot out the backside when she clicked on the flashlight icon, giving Kendra the confidence to go back to the kitchen to look for the big flashlight and latch the door.

The white beam from her phone lit her path well, but it also cast eerie shadows on the walls and around the living room. Kendra tried to remember where she put the lighter. She should have lit candles in her bedroom before she came out, but she hadn't thought of it. There were a couple of Yankee Candles on the mantle. Maybe she'd left a pack of matches next to them.

"I swear, Baxter. If you don't come this time, I will be so pissed," her words were loud in the dark house and bounced back to her from the walls. Kendra opened the door and flashed her phone light into the yard. "Baxter. Baxter, come home." A heavy ball of apprehension rolled in her gut. *Where was he?*

"He won't be coming home tonight." A deep, male voice spoke from approximately ten to fifteen feet behind her.

Kendra's muscles locked up with an initial deluge of adrenaline. She didn't move. "Where is he?" Her voice wavered.

"Not here." The man stepped toward her.

Cursing herself for leaving her gun in the bedroom, Kendra gripped her phone hard. She pressed the power and volume buttons simultaneously until her hand shook. An alert sound echoed in the darkness.

"Drop the phone." The man's tone was calm.

She'd have preferred to hear fear or uncertainty, even rage. Her mind raced, considering her options as she slowly lowered the phone toward the counter. Not knowing whether or not he was armed decreased her available options. Surprise was her best shot. Kendra spun around to face the intruder and crouched low. She shined the bright light into the man's eyes.

He deflected the beam, blocking it from his sight with one arm. He held something small in his hand that flashed in the light.

A syringe.

Chapter Twenty-Nine

A s soon as the door closed behind Lucinda, Rick turned and walked further along the street. The night was cool, and he flipped up the collar on his coat to keep the breeze at bay. He entered the park where he and Kendra had first kissed and he wished she were here with him now. Nerve endings pulsed, and he shivered as he made his way to "their bench". *God, when did I turn into such a sap?* He laughed at himself.

Rick sat there for a long time, gradually opening the doors in his mind that he'd kept firmly closed and locked for years. Images of the night Alyssa was killed assaulted him. He allowed his heart to slide into the emotional meat-grinder. It was time to deal with the past. He thought of his fiancée's beauty, her fiery temper, and her tender heart. "I loved you, Alyssa," he whispered. Tears he never released before slid down his cheeks and dripped onto the cement.

Eventually, after his emotion was spent, Rick wandered back to his apartment. The emptiness in his soul stretched open, ready to swallow him whole. He closed the door and toed off his shoes. A bourbon bottle stood on the counter, calling out to his sagging spirit. Rick dropped two ice cubes into a glass and splashed the Wild Turkey over them. He clicked on the TV, dumped himself on the hard rental-couch, and propped his feet on the coffee table.

Jimmy Fallon was signing off for the night. It was late. Rick knew he should go to bed, but that if he did, he wouldn't sleep. *Christ. When am I ever going to get past this shit?* He ran a hand over his face and took a gulp of his drink. The cold heat burned his throat and ignited in his stomach. He glared at the golden liquid. It wasn't helping.

His mind wandered over his ruined dinner with Kendra. She was so touchy about being respected as a female agent. Rick shook his head. The stupid thing about that was that every person at the Denver office knew how great she was. No one questioned her competency—but she didn't believe that.

Her insecurity combined with his over-active need to protect her blended together like vinegar and baking soda. Rick never thought he could care about another woman. It was too risky to open his heart again. But here he was, wanting to build something real, something lasting with Kendra. Only he had no idea how to overcome the combustion that inevitably happened between them. They'd talked about it. They both understood what was going on within themselves and each other, but still they seemed incapable of getting over it and moving forward.

It dawned on him that though it was true, both he and Kendra knew what their issues were, neither one of them had taken steps to deal with them. Kendra admitted she struggled with always fighting to measure up because of the way she was raised and the manner in which her family continued to treat her. But until she realized she didn't need their approval to succeed, she would always worry about what others thought. And as far as he went, Rick ran head-first into the fact that he'd never let himself grieve for Alyssa. He had kept her enshrined in his heart and refused to let her go. It was finally time.

With a burst of emotion, Rick jumped up from the couch and stalked to the kitchen. He dumped the remainder of his drink down the drain. On his way to the bedroom he felt his phone vibrate in his pocket. He tapped the screen and lifted it to his ear. "Sanchez here."

"Agent Sanchez?"

"Yes."

"This is the Douglas County Police Dispatch calling. We've received an SOS call from the cellphone of a federal agent by the name of Kendra Dean, but — "

Rick's abdomen flexed so hard it felt like someone had punched him. "What happened?"

"We don't have that information yet, sir. We've dispatched a unit to her home. They're in route. I called the after-hours line at the FBI Headquarters and they gave me your contact number. I must have gotten through to you before they did."

"I'm on my way." Rick disconnected the call and strapped his shoulder holster on. He checked his Sig's magazine and grabbed a spare as he sprinted to the front door. He ran to his car while dialing Kendra's number. The phone rang six times before Kendra's voice came over the line asking him to leave a message after the beep. "Shit!" His fear echoed against the cement walls of the garage.

The Explorer left black tire marks on the sidewalk outside the parking structure, the smell of burnt rubber acrid in the night air. Rick steadied his breath and focused on driving. He couldn't help Kendra if he got in a wreck. His phone connected to his car, and he called the Denver FBI headquarters.

"This is Agent Sanchez. I need you to contact Agents

Cameron and Stott. Let them know that Agent Dean sent out an SOS message from her phone and now cannot be reached. Tell them I'm on my way to Agent Dean's residence as back up and that I'll keep them apprised of the situation." Rick dialed Kendra's phone again, but it didn't ring at all. Instead, his call immediately transferred to the message system.

"God damnit!" He bellowed and pressed harder on the gas pedal.

Why did he leave her earlier? He was such an ass. Their argument had been so stupid—petty, each refusing to understand the other's nature. Why didn't he simply apologize for making her feel like he didn't think she could handle herself and explain again that it was more about his own sense of failure for not protecting Alyssa? If he'd swallowed his pride sooner, Kendra wouldn't be in danger now. He rigidly kept his imagination about why Kendra sent an SOS message to the police at bay, but his body rebelled. Bile mixed with bourbon bubbled up from his gut. The heartburn seared his esophagus.

Twenty minutes out, he gagged on his knowledge of what could be happening while he was helpless behind the wheel. An unreasonable burst of anger aimed at Kendra for living so far away, out in the middle of nowhere, exploded in his chest. He released the sense of helplessness with a growl.

That Kendra used the SOS on her phone rather than dial 911 scared the piss out of him. The most probable reason was because someone was with her and she had to disguise the fact that she called. Rick thanked God that she had her cell and could get the distress message out before... "Shit, shit, shit!" Rick slammed his hand against the steering wheel. The Explorer flew over the highway.

Chapter Thirty

✿

Kendra stared at the glistening needle in the man's hand. "What did you do to my dog?" she screamed.

He lunged toward her, but she leapt out of his way. The light she used to temporarily blind her attacker, also helped him to narrow in on her location. She clicked it off and dashed into the living room to the far side of the sofa, careful to keep the furniture between them. The moon lent enough glow that she could see him approaching her, step by agonizing step.

He stalked her, slowly circling the couch, "You can't run away from your sins, Agent Dean."

"What sins? How do you know my name?" Kendra's pulse thudded so hard, she struggled to draw breath. Her heart and lungs fought for dominant space in her chest. Kendra's back was to the fireplace. The intruder's was to the hallway. If she continued this circle game, when she edged to the other side of the sofa, she could make a break for it down the hall and get her gun. She stepped to the side, but the man didn't move.

Kendra worked to keep him talking. "Who are you? What do you want?"

"You know who I am—*and* what I want."

"I don't. I mean, I think you want to kill me, but I don't know why. I've never done anything to you." She glanced around the darkened room for something she could use as a weapon.

"You've been following me. Trying to get my attention. Tempting me." He took a step in her direction.

"Tempting you?" *He's insane.*

"I've seen you. I should have killed you the day we met. But, stupidly, I thought you were innocent." He crept another step.

Kendra glanced to her right, gauging the distance to see if she could make it past him fast enough.

He laughed. "Go ahead. Try it."

Her whole body trembled. "We've met?" She stalled.

His face twisted into an evil smirk and he reached behind to his back with his free hand. He pulled a gun out of his waistband. "Recognize this?" He pointed it at her.

A deadly chill shook her body. "Yes. I do. But you didn't kill me that day. You must have had a reason. What's changed?" Kendra shifted her weight, making ready to bolt.

"You wouldn't leave me alone. I saw how much you wanted me, and I knew if you got to me, you would drag me down into hell. That's when I realized you had to die. You're the same as your mother, Eve. Tricking and tempting her husband into death and destruction. Adam didn't deserve to be cast out of Eden."

He wasn't making any sense. Kendra figured he was slipping into psychosis, causing him to be even more dangerous. She wanted to run, but now that he had a gun in his hand she waited, considering how to get the weapon away from him without being injected with whatever clear concoction splashed inside the syringe. "So what's with the ribs? Why do you take them?"

"Isn't obvious? God took a rib from Adam to make a woman for him. But wickedness overwhelmed her, and she brought death and destruction to the world. Now, I'm avenging him. I am taking the bones back. When I get all the bones God sends me after, I'll be free."

"Why did you smash the women's skulls with a rock? They were already dead."

The man swung his head back and forth. "It's symbolic, don't you see? Adulterous and fornicating women must be sent out to the wilderness and stoned to death."

"And the wedding rings?"

"Two of those women were married. Can you believe it? Married and still on the prowl, enticing other men. It's pure evil and must be destroyed."

Kendra had to keep him talking. Maybe she could distract him by focusing on his self-imposed mission. "Did God tell you to come to Colorado?"

"I follow his guidance a step at a time."

"Why so many women in one place?"

A bright crazed gleam entered his eye. "That's *your* fault. If you would have let me go, I would have moved on. But you kept enticing me, following me, making me want you. The other harlots found me while I was waiting for you."

"But what did they do to you? What did they do that they deserved to die for?"

He cackled. "They tried to deceive me. To trick me—like you're trying to do right now!" He lunged at her.

Kendra's heart exploded, sending hot splinters through her body. She bolted toward the hallway. Half way down the hall his fingers scraped the back of her head. He grasped at her hair and clutched the collar of her robe. Kendra pulled the tie and slid out from the silk. She ran into her bedroom.

The man let loose a guttural scream filled with rage and sped after her. At the foot of her bed he caught her hair in his fist and twisted. Her phone rang and Abbot smacked the device out of her hand. It fell to the floor and he crushed it under the heel of his boot. He lost his balance, and they fell onto the mattress, his weight pinning her underneath him.

Crushed as much by not being able to answer her phone as by Abbot's weight, Kendra grasped for hope. Unable to move, she grunted. "Free from what? How will killing me make you free? God says, 'Thou shalt not kill.'"

His hot breath snaked down her neck. "I'm building a pyre of ribs. When I have enough fuel, I'll offer them as a burnt offering to God. He will forgive me and finally condemn all women. Women, since the time in Eden have led men to the grave. No longer will they be able to weaken men and make them helpless." He adjusted his body over hers, pressing out what little oxygen she held in her lungs. "My daddy, like Sampson, was strong—before my mother destroyed him and abandoned us. That will never happen to me. *You* almost overcame me. Even tonight, you caused me to sin."

"What are you talking about?" Kendra's words had no volume with so little air to push through her vocal cords.

"You know."

"I don't." She twisted her head around to pull in a slight breath, her lungs screaming for more. Fear pooled sharp and metallic at the back of her throat. "At least tell me your name."

"Abbot Lee—Avenger of Adam." He tossed the gun on the floor and swung the syringe to the side of her face. The movement offered Kendra a full inhale, but her limbs remained trapped.

"Abbot, please." With every drop of strength she had,

Kendra bucked and squirmed. "I haven't done anything to you. But for whatever you think I'm guilty of, I'm sorry."

He spit hot, rancid words into her ear. "The mouth of forbidden women is a deep pit; he with whom the Lord is angry will fall into it."

"It sounds like you're a man of faith." *A faith twisted beyond recognition.* She recognized bits of disjointed scripture and knew her only chance was to keep him ranting. "You've got it backwards, Abbot. God is about love and forgiveness. Doesn't God tell you to forgive others?"

"You are not truly repentant."

"I am! You could save me, instead of killing me. Talk to me." His body slackened and Kendra grasped at hope.

"Daddy warned me. Women will say anything to trick men."

"What else did your daddy tell you?"

"Women—Their throat is an open grave; they use their tongues to deceive. The venom of asps is under their lips. That is why you must die."

He shifted his weight again and the last thing Kendra saw was the syringe edging toward her neck.

Chapter Thirty-One

Rick cursed himself for not ordering a cruiser to sit outside Kendra's house. He knew the killer was circling her, he'd felt it in his bones. *Damn it!* Kendra would have been beyond pissed off if he had someone babysitting her, but she wouldn't be in whatever trouble she was facing now.

Images of Alyssa's murder flashed across the screen of his mind. They were relentless no matter how hard he worked to bat them away. His skin was cold and clammy, but his head burned. He willed himself to be at Kendra's but the laws of physics were against him. Rick pushed his foot to the floor. 95mph, 110mph, 120...

"Oh, God. Please. Please don't let her die. Please..."

Finally, he came to the turnoff to Sedalia. His tires squealed as he swerved off the exit ramp, blowing through a red light. No other cars were around this far out in the country in the middle of the night. Rick amended that assessment as a lone set of headlights approached him on the left side of the street. A truck drove toward him, whose driver forgot to dim his brights. Rick averted his gaze to the white line on the side of the road to avoid being temporarily blinded by the high-beams before he rushed on to Kendra's.

He screeched to a halt behind two Douglas County cop cars parked at her front walk in haphazard angles and jumped out. He ran to the first officer he saw, flipping open his ID and badge. "Agent Sanchez—FBI. Where's the woman who lives here?"

"Unknown." The uniform held a flashlight up to see Rick's ID. "Sorry, we're not taking any chances. We got an SOS call from a cellphone at this location. When we arrived, we found no one."

"What?" Every cell in Rick's body froze. His heart slowed and his senses numbed like he was inside a bubble. The words the officer spoke sounded far away. "Did you say no one is here?" Frigid horror sluiced down the length of his spine.

Another officer ran around the corner of the house from the left. "We found a dog!"

Rick skewered the young woman with a glare. "Where?"

She gestured for them to follow and jogged back the way she had come. Rick was on her heels in four long strides. Ahead were two officers crouched at the edge of a line of shrubs.

Rick's gut turned into wet sand, and he slowed his pace. *Baxter.* "Is he... What happened?"

One of the uniforms hovering over Baxter looked up. "He's breathing, but we need to get him to the emergency vet right away."

"Where's his owner?" Rick yelled.

Four faces turned to him. The officer he first spoke to when he arrived answered from beside him. "There is nobody in the house. There is one car, a Jeep Renegade, parked in the drive. Otherwise, it looks like no one is home. If it weren't for the dog, I'd think this was a prank."

"It's no prank. Get that dog to the vet right away. He's an

FBI K9, and he deserves the best." Rick sprinted into the house through the back door. The lights were off and there was no response from the switch. The ranking officer followed him inside. "What happened to the electricity?"

"Our guys were checking on that when they found the dog." The sergeant hollered out the door. "Find out what's going on with the lights."

Half a minute later, the lights snapped on. A female cop ran up the back steps. "The main breaker switch was flipped to off. Someone turned off the power intentionally."

Rick scanned the kitchen and living room. Nothing appeared out of place, so he ran back to Kendra's bedroom. The bedspread was rumpled and the tie of a flowered robe was lying on the floor. His eyes darted from one side of the room to the other, snapping to a halt on the nightstand. A pistol sat on top of a doily under the lamp. *What the hell?* Kendra would never leave home with her weapon lying out like that. *Where is she?* Rick's gaze fell to the floor where the remnants of a crushed cellphone were scattered across the carpet next to another gun. Relief knocked on the door of his mind but he refused to allow it in, remembering the killer didn't use guns. An image of Kendra's delicate neck with purple bruises crashed into his brain and he gagged.

An officer entered the room. "We've asked the neighbors if they heard or saw anything unusual tonight. So far, no one has."

Rick closed his eyes and let his mind float over the situation. The memory of the truck with its high-beams struck him as though the vehicle crashed into his body. He shivered and gritted his teeth to keep from throwing up.

"There was a car. Or a truck. Something—It passed me on my way here. The driver kept his brights on, so I don't know what kind of vehicle it was. Christ! Agent Dean has been kidnapped! We have to find her—now!"

He spun and ran for the front door. "Call it in. We have a murder suspect who drives a white van. Have all units on the lookout for a white, cab-forward van." Rick yelled over his shoulder on the way out the door.

He jumped into his Explorer, and peeled out, speeding toward town. His mind raced over possibilities. *Where would he take her?* No one knew this killer better than he did. The bastard always took his victims to the wilderness. They found the last two in the Chatfield State Park. The dog park...

He could be wrong, and if he was, it could cost Kendra her life. But Rick had to take the chance, it was the only solid idea he had. He called in for backup at the dog park near the south entrance to Chatfield. "And dispatch a K9 team too!" *Oh God, please don't let her die. Please help me get there in time.* He couldn't go through losing another woman he loved.

His brows crunched together. *Love? Do I love her?* "God damnit!" The word echoed in the car. "Hang on, Kendra. I'm coming."

Chapter Thirty-Two

꧁꧂

endra's head bounced on metal. She blinked her eyes open. *Where am I?* Groggy, she closed her lids and tried to draw her arm up to cushion her head. Her hand was stuck. She pulled harder. Kendra squeezed her lashes tight before blinking rapidly to clear her blurry vision. *What the hell?*

She struggled to discipline her mind to think coherently. How did she get here in this... was she in a car? No. Cars don't have metal floors. She drifted off, lulled on a wave.

Crack! Her skull bounced against something hard. Kendra's eyes flew open. It was dark, but she wasn't in her bed. A spike of adrenaline infused her blood and her heart slammed into her chest wall. A memory of her attacker slid through her blurry mind. She couldn't seem to grasp on to it, nor could she remember how she got wherever she was. But her body screamed an alert. Her life was in danger.

A thin rope dug into her wrists. She looked around. *Oh, God! I'm in the back of a van. Shit!* Awareness of her surroundings filtered in. She was tied, with her hands behind her. Her bound ankles and feet were bare. She shivered, and with the cold she realized she was wearing only her underwear and silk robe. Abbot must have put the thin cover back on her before he carried her out of her house. True terror sliced through her insides.

No one knows where I am. No one even knows I'm missing! If only she hadn't been so adamant with Rick, insisting she could take care of herself, he would have still been at her house. She wouldn't be in this mess. *Stop it! No time for that. THINK!* The van's cab was separate from the back cargo-area, so she could move without being noticed.

The road changed from pavement to a dirt road and the bouncing roughened. Kendra strained her neck to keep her head from smacking against the corrugated metal floor. She did her best not to focus on the plight of the other women who had taken this same ride. With her hands tied behind her, she tucked her knees up tight and stretched her arms down around her feet. Rope burns rubbed the skin on her wrists raw, but she wriggled until her hands were in front of her body. Even bound, that gave her a better chance to defend herself. She went to work on the knots tied around her ankles.

Kendra crawled to the door and tried the handle, but he had locked it. Kneeling, she peered into the dark interior, hoping to find something she could use as a weapon. There was an old metal milk crate in the back corner and she shuffled over to it. The van made a sharp turn and losing her balance, Kendra crashed into the side wall. After the first wave of pain receded, she regained her balance and rifled through the bin.

Inside, she found a roll of duct tape, a dirty coffee tumbler, motor oil, a funnel, and a dirty rag, but nothing helpful. The crate itself would hurt if she hit him with it, but it wouldn't stop him. The corner weld was rough though and Kendra rubbed the rope tying her hands across it, frantically working to fray it. Scraping her wrists in the process, she finally broke through.

With her hands free, she propped herself up against the side wall, to plan her next move. Her gaze rose to the roof. Across from her, attached to the top wall of the van, was a 2 x 4 plank with large hooks screwed in to it. A long orange extension cord hung from one, and the others each held three-inch-thick, trailer tie-down straps. She stared at the items, formulating a plan.

The van slowed and came to a stop. The engine died. A jagged, feral fear surged through Kendra's limbs and she shuddered violently. Taking a deep breath, she whispered firmly to herself. "Man up, Dean. You've always said you could take care of yourself, so prove it."

Kendra laid down, with rope loosely wrapped around her ankles, she held her hands behind her back, and closed her eyes, pretending to still be bound and unconscious. A key sounded in the lock seconds before the door slid open.

"We're almost there." Abbot spoke to her. He brushed her cheek with his fingers and her stomach contracted. Bile flooded her throat, it was all she could do not to react. Not to vomit.

Her captor pulled her across the floor, bent, and hoisted her over his shoulder. They were somewhere in the countryside. There were no buildings, cars, or street lights. Fortunately, the darkness concealed the item she gripped in her hands. Kendra played dead, though his shoulder dug into her belly. Abbot carried her a quarter mile or so, before he slid her body to the ground.

He turned away, looking for something, and Kendra silently rolled to her hands and knees, springing herself to her bare feet. She had braced a cargo strap under her arm and now gripped the metal ratchet with both hands. Behind him, she crept close. When he turned back, she surprised him by ramming the brass clip, as hard as she could upward, into his nose, smashing the bone. He screamed and his hands flew to his face. Blood oozed through his fingers and rage poured out of his eyes. Before he could reach for her, she followed the first hit with a solid kick to his balls.

The man collapsed to his knees and Kendra ran. She kept the coiled strap tucked tight under her arm. Not sure where she was, she looked for cover. Her best bet was to hide. She bolted back down the path that led to the van which she now saw was parked in a gravel parking lot. The signage and split-rail fence were familiar. *Of course!* He'd brought her to the dog park. Serial killers were usually creatures of habit and symbolism. It was often their greatest downfall.

Kendra sprinted as fast as she could, down the road. Her fear masked the pain from the sharp stones gouging her feet. She estimated that there was a campground about two miles to the north. If she could get there, before he caught her, she could scream for help. Behind her she heard him yelling. He was already up and coming after her. Kendra veered sharply to the left and dodged into the tree line and scrub, searching for suitable cover.

The sound of her attacker's feet pounding on the gravel drew closer. He was gaining on her. Fear powered her escape, but fury equally energized his chase. The biggest advantage she had over him was her training. She had to calm down and think.

Kendra tried to focus as she ran, but thoughts of her missed opportunity with Rick fought for space in her mind. She wished he knew she was here. She wished he could save her. Her damn pride had gotten too big again, and she pushed her best chance of happiness away. Now, in all likelihood, she would be killed. Her heart broke for the sense of failure and loss Rick would experience—again. "I'm so sorry," Kendra whispered into the dark.

The strap she held in her arm caught on a branch and yanked her back into the terror of the moment. Pulling on it to release, she stumbled and fell. Wearing only lace and a flimsy unbelted robe, her knees hit the dirt, and she slid on her bare belly, downhill fast. The ground fell out from underneath her and Kendra gripped the tie-down strap with all her might. Her feet dangled off the edge of... of what? A cliff? A ditch? A river bank? She wasn't sure and couldn't see.

Chapter Thirty-Three

Kendra pulled herself, inch by inch, back up to level ground, thankful she'd kept the strap. Otherwise, she would have run right over the drop off. She crawled to the foot of the tree that snagged her and leaning against it, she steadied her breath. As the adrenaline flooding her system eased, Kendra gained clarity, and a plan swirled through her mind.

She almost fell—so perhaps she could ensure that the bastard chasing her would. The depth of the hole was unknown, but it didn't matter. Even if it were only two or three feet, a sudden fall would certainly cause an injury and slow her would-be killer down. Kendra moved fast, tying one end of the strap to the base of the tree. Her fingers ached as they worked without the freedom of her wrists. She crossed the path, unrolling the tie-down as she went. Kendra felt around until she found a large shrub to secure the other end of the strap to. She stretched it tight about four inches off the ground.

Kendra closed her eyes offering a silent prayer, then grunted out loud to make it sound as though she fell. She darted behind a big boulder next to the shrub and listened. Heavy foot falls pounded the earth, running toward her. It took every ounce of self-discipline not to move—not to scream. If she ran, and he heard her, it might pull him off his path. Sweat trickled down her temple and she worried that even her perspiration made too much noise.

He was a mere ten feet away on the other side of the boulder, sprinting down the trail. She held her breath and gripped her hands into tight fists. Her nails pierced the skin of her palms.

His scream skidded up her spine and exploded in her brain. For long seconds silence reigned in the forest. Then she heard him hit the ground below. It was deeper than she thought, but Kendra didn't look.

She took off and ran parallel to the edge of the drop off. Her bare feet shrieked in pain from the abuse of the rough terrain. The road she expected to run into never came. She was turned around, disoriented. There were no footfalls chasing her or crunching through the underbrush, so Kendra stopped and braced her hands on her knees, panting. Her eyes darted in all directions. Nothing looked familiar. She was lost. If she ever got back to her K9 unit, she'd never hear the end of it. *The searcher got lost.*

Maybe her parents and Michael were right all along. Even with all her experience and training Abbot Lee took her captive from her own home. Now she was confused and helpless, wandering in the wilderness. Tears blurred her vision and a sob clogged her throat. She fell to her knees and cried. *Poor Baxter's dead, and soon I will be too. It's all my fault. Why couldn't I have settled for a smaller life? I should have listened to my family.*

Something deep inside Kendra's mind rebelled against her litany of doubts and her eyes dried up. "Get up, Kendra." She spoke the words out loud to herself. "Tears and self-pity won't help you right now. Stop listening to lies and remember your survival training. Keep moving. You can do this. You are capable, smart, and strong. You will survive."

The strength of her own words emboldened her. Kendra stared up at the sky, she might not know where she was on the ground but she could orient herself with the stars. When she gathered her senses, she noticed the stinging of the scraped skin on her hands, knees, and feet, but determined to ignore it. She pulled the thin robe tight around her body and stepped off, traveling north. Turning left, she hoped she'd come upon the campground she remembered, but if not, she would eventually run into the reservoir or a highway. Kendra set her path and pushed on, intently listening to the sounds of the forest behind her.

The moonlit reflection appeared to smooth out about fifty feet in front of her. As she neared the pool of moonglow, Kendra realized she'd found the road. *Thank God.*

As soon as she placed her first foot on the pavement, she sprinted toward help. An engine sounded behind her and she moved off to the dirt shoulder. She would flag the car down and ask for help.

The lights were on high beam, which though it made sense out here in the wilderness, set off a warning bell in Kendra's brain. She squinted and raised her arm to protect her eyes from the glare. When she did, Kendra recognized the white van—and it was barreling straight toward her.

She spun and raced up the road, preparing to dart across the strip of mowed grass at the side of the pavement and into the trees. The van's engine surged and Kendra knew that Abbot saw her. Tires squealed and she veered to her right toward a tangle of wild brush and scrub that grew along the edge of the woods. It was too thick to climb through, her bare feet a painful obstacle. The gorse scraped and pierced her calves and feet, leaving deep angry cuts and snagging at her robe. If she slowed down, he'd catch her and kill her.

Kendra ran up the edge of the thick wall of vegetation as fast as her legs could pump.

The van flew off the pavement and plowed into the row of bushes behind her. Temporarily stuck, Abbot spun the tires in reverse. Kendra used the opportunity to run back onto the road to gain distance.

She heard the van pull out of the ruts. He'd be on her in seconds. Rounding a bend, Kendra was blinded by flashing lights strung across the parking area and she tripped, falling again to her wounded hands and knees. Scrambling, gravel ground into her wounds which were on fire.

———

RICK STOOD ON HIS BRAKES. A WOMAN'S FORM silhouetted in the moonlight darted onto the road in front of his car and fell to the ground on her hands and knees. A lethal mixture of terror and relief doused his blood stream. Another unmarked car and two squad cars behind him, lights flashing, worked hard not to hit him or each other. Dust billowed into the night air. Rick threw open the door and sprang from his seat.

The shadow form collapsed to the ground. "Kendra?" Rick dashed to her side. He'd gathered her up in his arms before he thought to check her body for wounds. "I'm here. You're okay." He kissed her tangled hair. "I'm so sorry. Are you okay? Are you hurt?" Tears blurred his vision. She felt fragile and jittery, like a scared baby bird trembling against his chest.

Uniformed police officers rushed toward them and called to Kendra, "Where is he?"

Kendra wiped her face with the sleeve of her robe and peered up at Rick. He cupped her jaw in his hand and stared into her eyes. "Oh, God, Kendra. I thought..."

Her voice was weak, and she choked on a sob. "I'm okay." She gripped his arms, digging into his skin. "How did you find me?"

"It was just a guess. A fucking, lucky guess." He yelled to the officers. "Call an ambulance!"

"Already done. They're on their way, along with more back-up."

A large man with a big hairy dog rushed toward them, black in the glare of the lights. Rick instinctively pulled Kendra tighter into his body.

Tires screeched on the pavement behind them and Rick jumped up and turned, keeping Kendra in his arms. The white van sped straight at them. The driver's face was demonic in the glow of the dash. A shadow from his brow bone made his eye socket appear empty. Kendra screamed.

Rick lifted her, took two strides to this right, and dove out of the way, barely escaping the front fender of the van. He landed on his shoulder, tucking Kendra into his body, and absorbed the impact himself while protecting her from the fall. In a fluid movement, Rick released her and rolled to his knees while reaching for his gun. He aimed and fired three shots at the back of careening vehicle, blowing the left back tire.

The man with the dog sprang back as the white van sped by, barely missing them as well. He growled something in a guttural language that sounded something like "Gunner Dursch" and his dog bolted after the van. Rick canted his head to the side; not sure he could believe what he was seeing.

The dog took off after the crippled vehicle and quickly caught up. He leapt up to the driver's open window and latched on to the man's arm with a ferocious bite. He pulled back, his paws pushing against the door, and jerked the man from side to side. The man in the van screamed and attempted to pull his arm away only increasing the pressure in the dog's fierce tugging. He leaned out the window shrieking for someone to call the dog off and the shepherd looking K9 yanked him right out through the van window and held him in place on the ground.

Kendra pushed herself up from the grass. "Clay?" Her brows drew together and she leaned forward to see more clearly. "Gunner?"

The big man ran toward her. "I heard the call on the radio. Gunner and I came right away. Are you all right?"

"I'll be fine. Go, take care of Gunner."

Clay ran toward his dog and commanded him to release. In seconds a uniformed cop had a knee in the killer's back and was handcuffing him. Rick forced his muscles to unclench. He relaxed his tight grip on his pistol and rushed to Kendra's side. She reached up with both hands to his cheeks.

Rick searched her face and then her body. Only then did he realize she hardly had any clothes on, and he gently closed her robe. A sob escaped his throat.

Kendra leaned into him and wrapped her arms around his neck. "I'm okay, Rick. You got here in time. You saved me." She broke down then and cried.

He murmured into her hair, "Shh. You're okay. Thank God, you're okay."

Kendra pushed back from his chest and looked up. Her eyes were wild and Rick knew she was in shock. "He was in my house. He drugged me."

"I know, sweetheart. You're safe now."

"Baxter? Where's Baxter?" Her voice elevated and became shrill. "Is he dead? Did he kill my dog?"

"He's all right. Shh. Baxter will be okay. The cops found him in the yard and took him to the vet. He was drugged, but he's going to be fine." Rick didn't know for certain that was the case, but he went on faith.

"I got away."

"Yes, you did. You're incredible."

"He was chasing me. I ran a trip cord. He fell into a deep ditch of some kind. I thought that stopped him. But then he was in the van again..."

"Shh. Don't think about it right now. All that matters is you're safe. Let's get you into my car. Can you walk?" Rick scanned her body for any obvious injuries. Seeing blood on her knees and her torn up feet, he scooped her up in his arms and carried her. He opened the back hatch and sat with her on his lap. He took off his jacket, wrapped it around her shoulders, and waited for the ambulance.

Something cold and wet bumped his hand and Rick jumped. The fierce guard dog who just yanked a man from the van window sat down next to his leg, grinning up at him and panting. Involuntarily, Rick's body tensed.

The dog's handler chuckled. "Don't worry, he's perfectly friendly."

Rick glared at the guy. Friendly was not a term he would ever use to describe that dog. He scooted to the side to gain another inch of distance from the fangs.

Kendra leaned over and pulled the dog's muzzle up to her face. She kissed him and he rewarded her with several juicy dog-kisses in return.

"Good boy, Gunner. You got him, didn't you? You got that bad man."

The dog stood, wagging his whole back end and barked.

"That's right, Gunner. Good dog." Kendra looked up at the man on the other end of the leash. "I don't know how you got here in time, Clay, but if you and Gunner weren't here that bastard would have escaped to kill again."

"It's all in a day's work. I just answered the radio call." Clay's gaze bounced to Rick. He stuck out his hand. "Agent Sanchez, looks like you got your man."

"Jennings." Rick shook his hand. "We wouldn't have him without the help of your dog. What kind of dog is he? At first I thought he was a German Shepherd, but he looks different."

"He's a Belgian Malinois. Great dogs."

"I could see that. Remind me never to piss you off."

"Just take care of our girl here, and you won't have to worry."

"No problem there. Hey, I can't thank you enough for being here."

Clay patted Gunner's hip. "Just doin' our jobs. Besides, it looked to me like you got here first. If it weren't for you, that van would have run Kendra down."

Rick shuddered at the memory.

Chapter Thirty-Four

Rick watched the ambulance drive away carrying his precious cargo inside, blaring lights and sirens. The EMT assured him that Kendra had only superficial scrapes and bruises, but that they would give her a complete exam at the emergency room. He said they'd do blood work to determine the drug she'd been given as well. Kendra seemed to be stable, considering, and urgency wasn't necessary, but the lights and sirens were a sign of solidarity and respect. A second ambulance carried their prisoner along with two armed guards.

With bright LED spot lights, cops traced the path Abbot Lee chased Kendra down and searched for evidence. Another crime investigation unit started with the van, which by the looks of it would provide all the evidence they would need to connect the bastard to the murders, including a pair of bloody bolt cutters under the passenger's seat.

Cameron and Stott pulled into the parking area and stopped next to the crime scene tape. Rick met them at their car.

"Holy hell, Sanchez? Is Dean going to be okay?" Burke jumped out.

Rick nodded, trying to maintain professionalism though the catch in his voice gave him away. "Yeah, she's at the hospital."

"Good thing you got here in time." Burke gripped Rick's shoulder.

He shook his head. "Kendra got away from that fucker all on her own, even though she didn't have any weapons. All she had was a cargo strap. That bastard had at least a hundred pounds on her, too. God." He crossed his arms over his chest to keep from trembling. "When he tried to escape in his van, one of the dogs from Kendra's K9 Unit chased him down and yanked him right out of the window. Craziest thing I ever saw."

"Yeah, I thought I saw Jennings and his K9, Gunner." Burke gave Rick's shoulder a firm pat. "Kendra's always telling us she can handle herself. I guess she wasn't kidding." Burke lifted his chin toward a group of cops. "Looks like the crime scene investigation team has everything under control. Nothing more we can do here tonight. How about we go check on Dean?"

"Yeah." Rick thought for a minute he might be sick, and he bent over bracing himself on his knees. The reality of the night pressed heavily down upon him.

Burke gestured toward his partner. "Why don't you give Stott your keys? I'll drive, and he can follow in your car."

"Thanks." Rick tossed his keys to the man and let Burke walk him to the passenger door.

"The ride there will give you time to get a grip. You don't want to look like a pussy in front of the team's most bad-ass agent when we see her at the ER." Burke laughed and shoved Rick in the arm.

Rick smirked. "No, shit."

On their way to the hospital, the phone rang through Burke's car speakers. He pushed "Accept" on the dashboard screen. "Burke here."

"Oh thank God." A soft, feminine voice drifted throughout the interior. "I couldn't sleep so I was watching TV. I heard on the news that the police were searching for a kidnapped FBI agent in connection with the recent murders, and I thought..." A gulp sounded over the line.

Rick raised his brows at Burke and gave him a sly half smile.

Burke shrugged and grinned back. "Everything's okay, Susan. They got him. They got the bastard."

"Thank God! Are you all right? Was anyone hurt?"

"Yeah, I'm fine. I wasn't part of the chase. I showed up after it was all over. Listen, the cops will be contacting you. They'll need you to come in to identify the guy in a line-up."

"Of course. I'll do whatever I can." Susan paused. "So, does this mean we'll be able to start seeing each other now?"

Rick stifled a laugh, and Burke glared at him, mouthing, "Shut the hell up."

"Yeah. We should probably wait until after the trial to keep everything on the up and up. But then I'll take you somewhere special." A smart-ass grin spread slowly across his mouth. "In fact, maybe we could go on a double date with my boss and his girl—she's the agent who took the bastard down for him."

Rick flipped Burke off and laughed.

RICK SQUEEZED HIS EYES SHUT AND GROUND HIS TEETH against the memories of his last visit to an ER. He had held Alyssa in his lap, there was blood everywhere, but no more life within her. His body shuddered violently.

"Hey, man. Are you okay?" Burke slung his arm around

Rick's shoulders to steady him. "Kendra's going to be fine. She just had some scrapes and bruises, that's all."

"Yeah, I'm good." Rick sucked in a gulp of night air and released his fear. He needed to see Kendra, had to see for himself that she was alive and well.

They entered through the automatic doors and stopped at the reception desk. An exhausted nurse jotted notes on his clipboard. "Can I help you?"

Rick flashed his badge. "We're here to see Agent Dean."

A tired smile brightened the nurse's face. He pointed down the hall. "First door on the right. She's a trooper, that one."

"You can say that again. Thanks." Rick and Burke hurried to her room.

Three cops waited in the hall outside and two more were in the room with Kendra when Rick entered.

"I asked for Scooby-Do band-aids, but they refused." Kendra's voice was the only one he heard.

Rick rushed to the woman wearing a hospital gown, sitting on the bed with her hands, feet, and knees taped up with gauze. His eyes met hers and it seemed as though the rest of the room along with the police officers and nurses, simply dissipated into thin air.

He brushed his fingers over her cheek. "Hey, tough guy." His voice scratched over the lump in his throat. He blinked his eyelids against hot tears that blurred his vision.

"Hi." Her strong façade fell and her body trembled. A sob caught in her chest.

Rick gathered her into his arms, crushing her against his chest. "It's okay, baby. I got you. You're safe. You've been brave long enough. It's time to let it out now. I'm here." Rick pulled back just enough to look into her eyes. "I'm not going anywhere."

Chapter Thirty-Five

❧❀❧

The doctors and, more importantly, her SAC wanted Kendra to stay for another twenty-four hours in the hospital for rest and recovery. Rick and Burke spent that time tying up the ends of their case. The CSI team found a hand-scribbled receipt in Lee's van that led the agents to a dumpy, pay-by-the-hour or by-the-week motel.

Rick's lip curled as they pulled into the pot-hole ridden parking lot. Weeds grew through the cracks on pavement that might have once boasted fresh lines painted on it for parking spaces but now was a crumbling mess.

"Let's talk to whoever's in the office first." Rick pointed to a glassed-in lobby from the 1970s, which appeared as though that might also have been when the glass was last cleaned. Burke parked by the door. The agents stepped out of the car and scanned the area for possible trouble. It was nine o'clock in the morning, and since most criminals aren't early risers, the motel and its surrounding lot seemed quiet.

They entered the office and were immediately hit with a wall of stale cigarette smoke. The lobby was empty, no lights were on, but the bell on the door emitted an irritating electronic buzz. Rick peered over the counter to see if there was anything interesting on the desk, while Burke did a preliminary search of the space at large.

"You guys must be cops. What the hell do you two want?" A man who appeared to be in his late sixties waddled down a hall from a room in the back. He didn't bother to put on any clothes over his boxer shorts and stained wife-beater. The t-shirt was several sizes too small and his hairy gut protruded from under what was left of the hem.

"Good morning." Rick stared the man down. "I'm Agent Sanchez with the Federal Bureau of Investigation, and this is Agent Cameron. We'd like to ask you some questions about a guest you have registered here."

The old man laughed a raspy noise that caused his obvious emphysema to act up. He coughed up a mouthful of phlegm and spit into an unlined trash can next to the desk. "A *guest*, you say?" His mirth rumbled once again from his chest. "I'm not sure I'd call any of these assholes 'guests'. Besides, I don't know anything about any of them. They pay in cash up-front. The rest I don't want to know."

Rick drew a copy of Abbot Lee's mug shot out of his inside coat pocket. "Do you remember this man? We have reason to believe he is currently renting a room here."

Burke kept an eye out for movement outside or from any of the rooms while Rick asked the manager his questions. The old man rummaged through a desk drawer filled with miscellany and fished out a pair of readers. He rubbed the lenses on the filthy undershirt, shoved them onto this face, and squinted through them at the photo.

"Oh, yeah. That guy. I remember him."

"What do you remember about him?"

The man removed his glasses and raised his chin. He narrowed his eyes at Rick. "What's it worth to you?"

"Not as much as it's probably worth to you. You can

answer my questions here, or we can have you dragged in for questioning while we search every nook and cranny in this place to find what we need. Of course, I have no doubt we'd find more than we need for just this case. In fact, I wonder what else we'd discover?"

Shaking his head, the manager scratched his bare belly. "No need for that. I'll answer what I know, but it isn't much. Like I said, I stay out of my 'guests' business." He made air-quotes around the word. "I don't want to know what goes on behind those doors."

"How long ago did the man in the photo register for a room?"

The manager sighed and flopped into the desk chair. He flipped a switch on a computer monitor that Rick estimated was circa 1995. "This takes a few minutes to warm up."

Rick glanced at Burke who rolled his eyes. "All's quiet outside."

"Good." Rick braced his forearms on the counter and waited.

The computer keyboard was as grungy as the stubby fingers that jabbed at its sticky keys. "Okay. Here it is. Abbot Lee." The man glanced up at Rick. "No saying if that's his real name. I don't check. I don't—,"

"You don't want to know. I get it. What date do you have?

"He checked in about a month ago. Paid for one week. Since then, he's paid once a week. Cash. Hell, I don't even take credit cards. I'd never see any money if I did."

"Did you notice anything unusual about him?"

"No, all my 'guests' have their thing. All's I know is, he drives a dented up white van that he always parks in the back. Pretty average guy. He paid, I took his money. That's it."

"Okay. Will you show us his room?"

The old guy smiled revealing nicotine-stained teeth with

dark unfilled cavities evident. "Got a warrant, do you? Heh, heh."

Rick pinned the man with a glare. "Of course we do." He nodded at Burke who pulled the papers from his coat. "So, if you don't mind, we'd like you to take us to Lee's room."

Everything about the manager deflated except his engorged stomach, and he reached for his keys.

WHEN THE DOOR SWUNG OPEN, THE ROOM WAS DARK BUT for the stream of sunlight shining through the entrance. A rotten odor rolled toward the opening. Rick slid his hands into rubber gloves and he stepped inside. He flipped on the lights. "Leave the door open so we can breathe."

Burke coughed, wrinkled his nose and followed him inside.

Rick scanned the room. It was surprisingly tidy. The bed was made and there were no clothes on the floor. There was, however a white sheet spread across the carpet at the foot of the bed that was splattered with rust-colored drops Rick assumed was blood. At the edge of the sheet was an open wooden box.

Without stepping on the sheet, Burke bent over to look at the contents. "What the hell is that?"

"It looks like a cat-o'-nine-tails—a brutal whip used to flog prisoners a long time ago." Rick tilted his head and chewed his lower lip. "None of the victims had signs of this type of abuse."

"Shit, do you think there are other victims we don't know about?"

"Maybe, but two separate MOs? That seems unlikely. Especially because Lee was precise and methodical with his victims."

Rick carefully stepped around the sheet and made his way

to the back of the room toward the bathroom. The smell of decay was stronger there, and he took shallow breaths. He saw the reflection in the mirror on the wall behind the sink before he got to the clothes rack on the other side of the divider wall. His skin puckered with the sensation of centipedes crawling all over him. "Cameron, I've got something."

Burke hesitated for a breath before he followed. He stood frozen behind Rick's shoulder. "Oh my God."

"Yeah. Looks like we found his trophy case." They stared at an open suitcase sitting atop a luggage stand filled with bones. Each rib had pieces of tissue remaining, in varying degrees of decay, presumably correlating to the time that had passed since they were removed from their bodies.

A bitter lump of realization pressed down on Rick's chest. He and Burke stood staring at over ten bones. To his knowledge there were only seven victims. Where were the others? He closed his eyes.

"Looks like we still have an open case."

Chapter Thirty-Six

Kendra ended up staying the rest of that night and one more in the hospital. Baxter went home the day after the attack as soon as he slept off his dose of Rohypnol. The morning they released Kendra, Rick brought Baxter with him to pick her up. She was waiting for them, dressed and ready to go in a wheelchair she insisted she didn't need or want, but that the nurse demanded she be rolled out in.

"Hey, sweet boy!" She bent forward and let Baxter lick her face. "You poor guy. You've had a rough go, haven't you?" She stroked his head and ran her hands over his soft ears. "It's all over now though, and you can ease back into a luxurious retirement."

Rick crouched down next to her dog and gazed up at her, his obsidian eyes holding buckets of emotion. "How are you doing? Ready to go home?

She reached for his hand and squeezed. "Beyond ready. Get me outta here."

. . .

ONCE HOME, RICK INSISTED ON CARRYING HER INTO THE house. Kendra argued. "I'm not an invalid. Put me down."

"Tomorrow you can go back to being a tough guy, but today you're going to humor me and let me take care of you. I saw your feet. They were scraped raw. Let's give them a chance to heal."

"Oh, brother." Kendra scoffed, but she slid her arms around Rick's neck and allowed herself to enjoy the closeness of his body and his soft breath on her cheek.

He propped her up on the sofa and brought her a fresh, hot cup of Earl Grey tea.

Kendra blew on the surface and took a sip. "Oh, that tastes good."

Rick smiled and handed her a slim white box from the counter. "Oxley insisted you get back online right away." He opened the box and handed her the slim silver device. "It's all set for you to restore your data."

"Figures. No rest for the weary." She took the new phone and turned it on, uploading her backup while Rick made lunch. Kendra cast her gaze around the room, remembering the last time she was there was with Abbot Lee, the man who wanted to kill her. She drew in a deep breath and went through each moment. She didn't relive the fear, but rather studied the scenario and considered her actions.

"You look deep in thought." Rick set a tray filled with sandwiches, chips, a bowl of grapes, and a plate of chocolate-chip cookies down on the coffee table. "Are you thinking about that night?"

She nodded. "I am. My biggest mistake was not trusting my gut. I thought I heard someone, but then I talked myself out of it. Because of that, I left my weapon in my bedroom. If I would have kept it with me, none of the rest of it would have happened."

"Kendra, you can't second guess yourself. You were amazing." He sat on the floor next to the table facing her and wrapped his arms around his knees. "I'm the one who screwed up. I should have never left that night. I was mad, but so what? I should have stayed and talked things through." He dropped his chin. "I knew it as soon as I got in my car, but I was too proud to come back inside."

Kendra's heart softened, and she reached for his hand. "I was just as prideful. I thought the same thing while I was bouncing around in the back of the van. If only I hadn't told you to leave. I'm sorry, Rick. The truth is, I completely understand why you feel protective. I feel awful about your losing your fiancée the way you did. I can't imagine that kind of pain."

Rick leaned forward, lifted her hand and kissed her skinned knuckles before he rose to his knees and took her face in his hands. "I don't know what I would have done if I had lost you. I was terrified."

"Me too. But, we're here now. Let's make the most of it."

Rick smiled and met her lips with the tenderest of kisses.

AFTER LUNCH, KENDRA SLEPT. SHE WOKE TO HER PHONE buzzing from somewhere in her covers. She jiggled the quilt until the device fell out and she looked at the screen. *Michael*.

"Hey, Mike. What's up."

"Kendra, my God. I just heard what happened. The serial killer story is all over the news. They aren't releasing the names of any of the police or FBI, but the woman that psycho abducted was you, wasn't it?"

"Calm down, Michael. Yes, it was me, but I'm fine, and we got him."

"Mom's been calling me all morning, but I've been dodging her. I wanted to talk to you first."

Kendra sighed, wondering for the millionth time why her

mom didn't just call her. "Well, now you can tell her you talked to me and I'm fine."

"Can I tell her you've finally decided to quit your job? That's the only thing she'll want to hear."

Kendra bit her lip and considered her answer. "You know what, Mike? When you talk to Mom, I want you to tell her that if she wants to say something to me, she can call me directly. And as far as my job goes? Here's the deal. Seven women were kidnapped and killed. I was also abducted, but because of my training and experience, I was able to escape *and* we caught the bastard. So, no. I am not quitting the FBI. In fact, I'm getting a new K9 partner next week. I hope you'll come up soon to meet her."

Silence ticked by like a grandfather clock. Kendra waited. A full minute later, Michael spoke. "Okay. You know, you're right—about Mom *and* your job. The truth is, though it scares the crap out of me, I'm really proud of you."

Tears pricked her eyes. "Thanks, Mike. I've wanted to hear that for a long time."

"I should have said it sooner. I love you, Ken."

"Back at you."

"Hey, is that Sanchez dude still hanging around?"

Kendra lifted her gaze to Rick who was sitting in an over-stuffed chair watching her. She smiled. "Yeah, he's still hanging around."

"Well, you tell him I meant what I said. The next time I come to Denver I want it to be for a nice visit, not to have to kick his ass."

Kendra laughed aloud at the image of her smaller and substantially softer brother trying to beat up the rock of a man sitting across from her. "I'd hate for you to have to teach him a lesson, Mike. I'll be sure to tell him."

Rick grinned and shook his head. "Tell Mike not to worry. I keep my promises."

. . .

AN HOUR LATER, KENDRA'S PHONE BUZZED AGAIN. FACE Time—it was her mom. She rolled her eyes at Rick and pressed the button. "Hi Mom."

"Oh, honey! Michael called and told me all about what happened to you. Are you going to be all right?"

"Yes, mom. I'm fine. Just a few scrapes and bruises. The good news is a serial killer is behind bars."

Her mother started to cry and held a tissue over her face.

"Mom, don't cry. I'm fine, I promise."

Her mom shook her head and then the screen wobbled sending disjointed images of her parents' living room ceiling, carpet, and her dad's shoe. Next her dad's concerned face peered at her through her phone.

"Kendra? It's Dad."

She smiled. "I can see that. We're on Face Time."

His brows scrunched together. He'd never be comfortable with new technology. "Right. Michael tells us you are okay."

"Yes, I'm fine. A few scrapes, that's all."

Her dad stared at her through the screen. His jaw worked and his lips twitched. He nodded once as though he'd finally decided something. "Kendra, I want you to know I couldn't be prouder of you. You've done an incredibly brave thing and other women are safe today because of you."

Kendra's jaw dropped open wide, and she blinked. Rick moved to her side and squeezed her shoulder. She glanced at him and then back at the screen.

"Is that Agent Sanchez there with you?"

"Yes, but how..."

"Your brother keeps us up to date." Her father glared at Rick for long seconds.

"Nice to meet you, sir. I'm Rick Sanchez."

"Yes, well. I'd rather meet you in person, so I could shake

your hand. Sounds like you two make a good team. I expect you to take excellent care of my little girl."

Rick smiled at her father. "Yes, sir. Though, she does a fine job of taking care of herself."

Her dad nodded. "You're right. She certainly does." His gaze moved back to Kendra. "I love you, Kendra Sue."

"I love you too, Dad."

Tears of joy spilled out of her eyes and after she clicked off the call, Kendra sat stunned. Her chest expanded like a hot-air balloon. "Was that real?"

Rick grinned at her. "I believe it was."

OVER A SIMPLE DINNER OF CHEESE AND SPINACH OMELETS with toast, Rick told Kendra what he and Burke found when they investigated Lee's motel room.

"There are three more bodies?" Kendra went cold. "Any idea where he left them?"

"We're running a search on missing persons in Tennessee, Kentucky, Illinois, Missouri, Kansas, and Colorado."

"That's a lot of territory to cover."

"True. We'll start hitting it hard tomorrow. I'm just glad Lee's behind bars and won't be hurting anyone else."

"They aren't wasting any time prosecuting him."

"No, and the sooner the better as far as I'm concerned." Rick slathered butter on his toast. "Your cupboards are almost bare, Mother Hubbard. Want me to swing by the grocery store for you tomorrow?"

Chapter Thirty-Seven

Weeks later, Rick sat next to Kendra on her back deck watching the lazy sun dip behind the foothills. Clouds shot through with streaks of golden-glory wisped across the horizon. Baxter and Annie lay together in the shade of a lilac bush resting from their recent game of bark and chase.

Kendra and Rick finally shared the beer and barbecue they started on the fateful night of her kidnapping. Peppered steaks sizzled on the grill. He tapped her bottle with his. "*Salud*."

"Cheers." She propped her feet up on a chair next to her and pointed her chin out to the yard. "I'm so glad to see those two becoming such good friends. Baxter is smitten."

A slow smile spread over Rick's mouth. "There's something about the females in this house. I can't explain it." He reached across the table for her hand and they sat in the quiet comfort of the early evening, reveling in the fortune of being together.

"Burke called me today."

"Yeah? What'd he want?

"He said something about going with us on a double date with him and Susan Bell. Isn't she the woman Abbot Lee attacked in the grocery store parking lot?"

Rick laughed. "Yes. I should have sent you with Burke to interview her that day. He went alone and ended up falling in love."

"What?"

Rick shrugged. "He's head over heels."

He rubbed his thumb over Kendra's knuckles. "Final ruling from the court came down today. Lee was convicted of nine murders and sentenced to eight consecutive terms of life imprisonment." Rick sat forward and reached across with his other hand, holding hers in both of his.

"Why only eight life terms?"

Rick shook his head. "Plea deal. Lee confessed to two other murders and gave us the location of their bodies." He barked a laugh. "Some plea deal. It doesn't give him anything. But I'm not complaining."

"But that still leaves one murder. Is he saying he didn't commit that one? I thought there were ten ribs?" Alarm pinged through her like a pinball.

Dark eyes studied her before they moved to the sunset. "The tenth was his mother's." Rick took a second before he continued. "Apparently, Lee's father taught him how to remove ribs, using his own mother's body. He told Lee that God had ordained him to go out in the world and avenge Adam."

Heart sick, Kendra nodded, but a sense of frustration tightened her gut. The sentence didn't seem like enough punishment. His life in prison in exchange for nine lives lost and the grief of nine families? "Even eight life sentences doesn't really feel like justice. But, at least we caught him."

"*You* caught him, Kendra. I'm still stunned by your bravery."

Kendra smiled at him. She'd dealt with a lot of issues out there in the dark the night Abbot Lee tried to kill her. For the first time in her life, she was pleased to hear that someone she cared about was proud of her, but she no longer *needed* to hear it. She was proud of herself, and she knew she could handle what life threw at her. She was good at her job and loved every minute of it. "Thanks, but it was really Clay's K9, Gunner, who apprehended him. That dog's a total bad-ass."

Her gaze slid from the hungry promise in Rick's dark eyes to the temptation of his lips. He smiled knowingly, and she bit her lip. Her pulse kicked up a notch.

"So what's next for you?" he asked.

Kendra called to her dogs. "I'll be in intensive training with Annie for a couple more weeks. Bax and I are still getting used to sharing our space at home with her. Baxter is teaching that girl all his tricks, aren't you boy?" Baxter hopped up the steps, moving to his favorite spot by her feet. He licked her hand before settling down with his chin resting across his front paw. Annie followed, and curled up beside him.

"I have a few tricks I could teach you, if you want." Rick's eyes caressed her curves.

"Is that so?" She smiled at his innuendo but returned to the original subject. "What about you?" Kendra tried to sound casual, as though Rick's plans didn't matter to her. "What's on your horizon?"

"You mean after tonight?" His simmering gaze reached deep inside her and flipped a switch.

She swallowed hard. "Yeah, *after* tonight…"

A regretful smile softened his intensity. "I have to go back to Chicago." His shoulders curved and his gaze fell to the table.

Kendra rolled her lips in and bit down, nodding. "I figured you would. When do you leave?"

"Tomorrow."

"So soon?" Kendra's heart pinched. She set her bottle next to her plate and reached again for Rick's hands.

He clasped her fingers and pulled her over to him. She got up and moved around the table. He settled her on his lap. "We'll figure something out."

Kendra cupped his jaw and kissed his forehead. "Promise?" She slid her fingers over his cheek and combed them through his jet-black hair. Wanting to lose herself in the fathomless depth of his dark, sparkling eyes, she bent down and kissed his mouth. His body shifted under her and his hand dove into the length of her hair, twisting and tangling. He pulled her tight, deepening their kiss.

They parted, breathing hard, and Kendra slid from his lap to stand. Pulling his hand, she stepped toward the house.

His voice was hoarse. "The steaks?"

"Turn off the grill."

"You sure?"

One side of her mouth rose in a half-smile. "I've always been sure. How about you?"

Rick sprang to his feet to follow her and turned off the gas. Once they were inside, he pulled her into a toe-curling kiss. He ran his tongue along her jaw, nipping and kissing his way down her neck. Kendra tilted her head back to get more and Rick groaned. He slipped one arm around her shoulders, the other under her knees and lifted her. His lips traveled over her skin as he carried her down the hall.

Gently he laid her on the bed. His gaze, sizzling with desire, never left her as he reached back and pulled his shirt off over his head. His bronze skin glistened in the waning sunlight. The beams cast dark shadows accentuating the hills and valleys of his muscled torso. Kendra sucked in a breath. He was Adonis.

Rick stretched out next to her on the bed. His gaze reading her wanton thoughts. He grinned and began his sensuous ministrations on her neck, his hand caressing her through her clothing. Kendra, slid her hands down his back and pulled him close. Impatient to feel his skin against hers, she unbuttoned the first button of her top.

He brushed her hand away. "Let me. I want to take my time."

"You're killing me."

He chuckled. Kissing her, twisting his tongue around hers, he spoke into her mouth. "That's my intention."

The fire in his eyes ignited a white-hot flame inside of her and she reached for his belt. His passion took over and his patience flew away with the rest of his clothes. Rick fumbled with buttons that separated them, popping the last two. Kendra shimmied out of her lacey underwear and he consumed her. Lights flashed behind her eyelids and her breath came fast. She arched her back to get closer, to get more.

Dizzy with euphoria and elation, she gripped the bedspread with one hand and the back of his neck with the other. Slowly, she drifted, returning to earth. When she opened her eyes, he was staring into them.

He gave her a bashful grin. "Sorry."

Disoriented, she blinked? "What? What could you possibly be sorry for?"

He dropped his gaze, his thick lashes black against his swarthy cheeks. "I sort of lost control. Give me a minute. Next time, I'll go slower." He looked back into her eyes. "I meant to, but you drive me crazy. I..."

"You were perfect."

He studied her for a long moment. "*We're* perfect."

Kendra nodded, knowing the simple truth of his statement. "So, what are we going to do?"

Rick gazed at her hesitating.

"What's going on in that handsome head?"

"I hope this will make you happy." He ran a hand over his face. "I put in for a permanent transfer to Denver and it came through this morning."

Kendra was stunned. "You're moving here?" Champagne bubbles flowed through her veins and she felt giddy. "But you said you had to go back to Chicago."

"I do. I have to tie up some loose ends and pack my stuff, but that shouldn't take more than a couple of weeks." He cocked his head and gave her a timid smile. "So... good news?"

Kendra threw her arms around his neck. "It's great news!"

He nuzzled her neck. "I'd hoped you say that."

"What about Jack? How does he feel about losing his partner?"

"He's completely focused on Laurel these days. Last I heard he was over in Scotland. I don't know what his plans are, but either way, my plans are to move to Denver." Rick drew back and stared into her eyes. "I love you Kendra Sue Dean. I'd like to make a life with you."

Warmth glowed throughout Kendra's body and she was overwhelmed. Her eyes blurred with tears of joy. "I love you too, Ricardo Mateo Sanchez."

THANK YOU SO MUCH FOR READING *AVENGING ADAM*. I hope you loved getting to know Rick and Kendra! The next book in the FBI-K9 Series is Burke and Susan's story, but Rick and Kendra play a role too in Body Count!

· · ·

BUT, BEFORE YOU GO, IT WOULD ABSOLUTELY MAKE MY DAY if you would take a minute to write a quick review on Amazon. Thank you!

~ Jodi

Review Avenging Adam

GET **BODY COUNT** ~ THE NEXT BOOK IN THE FBI-K9 Series now!

Body Count
Book 2 ~ FBI K9 Series

Abducted and hidden away deep in the Rocky Mountains, Susan Bell is frantic to escape her murderous captor.

Freshman Special Agent Burke Cameron is straight-laced, traditionally minded, and comes with a hefty set of old-fashioned values. Burke doesn't know what to do with the free spirited, progressive woman he's falling for. He and Susan don't want any of the same things and he knows he should move on, but he can't seem to resist her.

Burke and Susan's world views are polar opposites and a lasting future together is impossible to imagine. But when a group of six women, including Susan, goes missing in the Colorado Rockies, their differences fall away, and all that matters to Burke is finding her.

He enlists the help of his friend, Agent Kendra Dean and her FBI-K9 partner, Annie. As soon as they are on the trail, they realize they're not simply searching for lost women— they are tracking a killer. They discover one body after another.

Desperate to rescue Susan, Burke prays that the next body they find isn't hers.

Stay up-to-date on all my new releases and other news. Join my mailing list!

or

Visit my website at Jodi-Burnett.com

Also by Jodi Burnett

Acknowledgments

Thank you to all the many wonderful folks who supported me and encouraged me during the writing of Avenging Adam. I would especially like to thank Officer J. Villalva and his wife who patiently answered my questions and filled my imagination with stories of brave and valiant police officers and their K9 partners. Thanks also to a particular FBI-K9 Agent who is the brother of a fellow author, T J Logan. He not only took the time to answer my questions but more importantly spent years dedicating his life to keeping this country safe. As always, I'd like to thank my beta-readers and editors for helping to shape and polish all my words.

About the Author

Jodi Burnett is a Colorado native. She loves writing Suspense Thrillers from her small ranch southeast of Denver where she also enjoys her horses, complains about her cows, and writes to create a home for her imaginings. Inspired by life in the country, Jodi fosters her creative side by writing, watercolor painting, quilting, and crafting stained-glass. She is a member of Sisters In Crime, and Rocky Mountain Fiction Writers.

Jodi-Burnett.com

Made in the USA
Las Vegas, NV
23 January 2023